Dawn

Diary Three

Other books by
Ann M. Martin

P.S. Longer Letter Later
(written with Paula Danziger)
Leo the Magnificat
Rachel Parker, Kindergarten Show-off
Eleven Kids, One Summer
Ma and Pa Dracula
Yours Turly, Shirley
Ten Kids, No Pets
Slam Book
Just a Summer Romance
Missing Since Monday
With You and Without You
Me and Katie (the Pest)
Stage Fright
Inside Out
Bummer Summer

THE KIDS IN MS. COLMAN'S CLASS series
BABY-SITTERS LITTLE SISTER series
THE BABY-SITTERS CLUB mysteries
THE BABY-SITTERS CLUB series
CALIFORNIA DIARIES series

California Diaries #11

Dawn

Diary Three

Ann M. Martin

SCHOLASTIC INC.
New York Toronto London Auckland Sydney
Mexico City New Delhi Hong Kong

ISBN 0-590-02389-6

12 11 10 9 8 7 6 5 4 3 2 1 9/9 0 1 2 3 4/0

Printed in the U.S.A 40

First Scholastic printing, February 1999

For Betsy Howie

Dawn

Diary Three

Late Friday night 2/5

Ah. The weekend. Here at last. I don't know why I'm so thrilled. It's not like I have plans or anything. It's just a nice break. This is such a draggy time of year. Even in California. We don't get all that snow and ice and slush we used to have in Connecticut, but we've had endless storms and rains and

Oops. Sorry. Gracie was crying. Now I'm back. I'm baby-sitting tonight. These are my big Friday night plans. Baby-sitting for Gracie and Jeff.

This has been the great excitement of the week: On Tuesday the groundhog saw his shadow, so we will have six more weeks of winter. Big deal.

I can never understand how that groundhog thing works. Year after year it mystifies me. What is that groundhog's name? Punxatonnie Slim? (I think he resides in Pennsylvania.) And why does seeing his shadow mean a longer winter? If he sees his shadow, doesn't that mean it's a nice sunny day? And wouldn't *that* mean that we're already enjoying an early spring? Very strange.

Oh, well. I don't think Punxatonnie Slim's condition in Pennsylvania has all that much to do with California weather anyway.

Boy. Gracie is really fussy tonight. Maybe she's getting new teeth. I've decided to keep her up with me for awhile. Now she's on her tummy on my floor, examining the bunnies on her blanket. She seems a lot happier, but I MUST get her back in her crib before Dad and Carol come home. They won't appreciate my laid-back baby-sitting techniques. They — Yikes there's their car

Later Friday night 2/5

Whoa. That was close. I scooped Gracie up and ran her back to her room. When Dad and Carol came in, they found me standing over Gracie's crib in the dark, talking softly to her, like I'd been trying to soothe her for hours. But I just know that letting her get up is better for her. If I were a baby, that's what I'd want.

Oh, well.

Dad paid me, and now he and Carol have gone to bed, so I'm the only one up. I can't sleep. I'm rolling that groundhog issue around in my head, which is absolutely insane. Whenever I start mulling over something as idiotic as a groundhog, I _know_ something else is really bothering me. What is really bothering me tonight?

Easy.

It's Sunny.

We're still barely speaking to each other.

I AM SO MAD AT HER.

And yet she's my friend. She's been one of my _best_ friends for so long. I miss her. I miss her a lot.

I'm mad at her and I miss her.

Saturday 2/6

I'm sitting in my bedroom, looking out the window and across the yard at Sunny's house. It's bad enough being mad at your best friend, but when she lives right next door, it's just so . . . uncomfortable.

I wonder if Sunny feels the way I do. Possibly, this doesn't matter to her just now. After all, her mother is back in the hospital. In, out, in, out, for how long? The last year or so, at least.

I hope I never get cancer.

Sunny spends a lot of her time and energy <u>not</u> visiting her mother in the hospital. She must have to go to great lengths to appear so busy that, day after day, she can't get to the hospital.

I think <u>I'll</u> visit Mrs. Winslow today.

This afternoon.

Later Saturday afternoon 2/6

Oh. My. God.

Mrs. Winslow looks dreadful. Absolutely dreadful. Her hair was _just_ starting to grow back and then they began chemo on her again, and now it's coming out in brushfuls. I brought her a new scarf today so we could experiment with styling. She tied it on her head so that just a few wispy bangs were showing.

"How should I fix these, Dawn?" she said. She was looking at her bangs in a hand mirror and holding up a comb.

"Maybe sort of over to the side," I suggested.

So she ran the comb through the bangs and pulled them out. I mean, _all_ the bangs. Clean out of her head.

I nearly cried.

But Mrs. Winslow just held up a big pair of gold hoop earrings and said, "Well, if I want the pirate look, it'll work better with_out_ the bangs." And then she dropped her bangs into the wastebasket (on top of another clump of hair).

I forced a laugh. "The pirate look. Oh, that's your best look."

Mrs. Winslow set the comb and mirror aside. She put on the earrings. "How's Gracie?" she asked.

"Teething," I replied.

"Oh, poor you. Poor all of you."

"Jeff got up in the middle of the night and slept on the kitchen floor," I told her. "He tried the bathroom first, but the kitchen was farther away from Gracie's room. Anything to escape the screeching. I slept with my headphones on."

"Smart girl," said Mrs. Winslow.

I really wanted to ask if Sunny had been by recently, but I didn't say anything. I didn't want to put Mrs. Winslow in the middle. She knows Sunny and I aren't speaking (much), and she feels bad about it. She also feels hurt that Sunny visits her so rarely. But she doesn't mention it. At least not to me. After all, Sunny is her daughter.

I tried to make myself useful. I watered Mrs. Winslow's flowers. I tidied a pile of newspapers and magazines and set them under the visitor's chair. Mrs. Winslow is lucky to have a private room, but god it's tiny. You can barely walk around her bed. The rest of the furniture consists of a narrow table that slides across the bed so she can eat (which she hardly ever feels like doing), the visitor's chair (just _one_), a TV, which is bolted high up in a corner of the room and is really hard to operate, and the wastebasket. That's it. I tidied up in, like, 45 seconds. After that I filled the water glass and got Mrs. Winslow another blanket. (She's cold all the time.) By then I was starting to get nervous that Sunny might show up after all, and I really didn't want to run into her.

I put my jacket on. "So how long do you think you'll be here this time?" I asked.

Mrs. Winslow shrugged. "I never know. Awhile, I guess."

I nodded. Then I kissed her cheek, said good-bye, and left.

You know what? This is completely ridiculous, but every time I kiss Mrs. Winslow this teeny, tiny part of me wonders if you can catch cancer. I know you can't.

And still I wonder.

Saturday night 2/6

I love Ducky. I really do.

When I came back from the hospital, I walked by the Winslows' house and saw him sitting on their front porch.

"Hey, Ducky!" I called.

"Hey," he replied. He stood up.

"What are you doing?" I asked.

"I dropped by to see if Sunny was home. I guess she isn't"

I love Ducky, and Ducky loves Sunny. Deeply. Like a sister. And I love him like a brother. Well, that's not quite true because I do not feel the way about Ducky that I do about Jeff. (Although maybe that's because Ducky is sixteen and Jeff is ten.) What I'm trying to say is that there is no boyfriend/girlfriend thing going on between me and Ducky, or Ducky or Sunny. Ducky just loves Sunny and me. Maggie and Amalia too. He likes to take care of his friends. He's especially protective of Sunny right now.

Ducky trotted across the Winslows' lawn.

"I was just at the hospital," I told him.

"With Mrs. Winslow?"

"Yeah."

"Was Sunny there?"

"Ducky."

Ducky shrugged. "Just asking."

I said, "A, she hardly ever goes to the hospital. And B, we still aren't speaking, so we certainly wouldn't have gone to the hospital together." I took off my baseball cap and put it on Ducky's head.

"I just thought you might have run into each other there."

"Nope. Want to come over?"

"Sure."

Ducky and I sat at our kitchen table and split a bottle of spring water. Carol joined us for awhile. She sat down on the other side of the table and began to breast-feed Gracie. Ducky hasn't been to my house that often, so he doesn't know Dad and Carol very well. But this didn't stop Carol. She didn't even hesitate before lifting up her shirt. At least she kind of rearranged herself and Gracie's blanket so that not TOO much of her breast showed. And Ducky barely batted an eye. He didn't look, and he didn't make a big deal about _not_ looking. He is incredible that way.

I kept telling myself that breast-feeding is a natural bodily event.

But really. In front of my friends?

Eventually Carol and Gracie left. Ducky and I paged through _The Corner Bulletin_, which is the new community newspaper. (It's, like, 8 pages long.)

"Hey, look! Vanish is going to be

playing next week. At the high school in Verona."

"Cool. They're advertising now," said Ducky.

And at that very moment, almost as if she'd overheard us, Amalia called. I picked up the phone, heard her voice, and shrieked. "We just saw the notice about Vanish in the newspaper!" I cried. "How come you guys are playing in Verona?"

"Hey, we have a reputation now," Amalia said. "People know us. The offers are pouring in."

We chatted for a few minutes and then hung up.

Ducky left.

I was at loose ends. I called Maggie. Ostensibly I was calling just to say hi, but I tried to work food into the conversation. I wanted to hear Maggie say she'd been eating like a normal person lately, or that she had gained five pounds and needed to buy new clothes. Something. But she didn't pick up on my cues. I guess I was too subtle. Anyway, she's much better these days. Dr. Fuentes is really helping her work things out.

When I hung up the phone this time, I just sort of sat at the table. I thought about what a weekend in Stoneybrook, Connecticut, would have been like — Mary Anne and Claudia and Stacey and everyone in and out of the house, baby-sitting, so many activities that by the end of the weekend I would need another weekend just to recover.

So many activities? What I really mean is so many friends. So many close friends. I don't seem to have that now. Not with everything changing.

Not without Sunny.

Sunday 2/7

Guess what. I took off on my bike for a ride this afternoon, and when I got home, Sunny was darting across our backyard in the direction of her house. I found Carol and Gracie in the kitchen and two bottles of spring water on the table. Now, Gracie certainly wasn't drinking that bottled water. So I said, "Carol, was Sunny just here?"

Carol looked uncomfortable, but she replied, "Yeah. She came over to visit Gracie."

"She has awfully good hearing," I commented.

"Gracie?"

"No, Sunny. She's fast too."

"What do you mean?" asked Carol.

"I mean that she must have zipped out the back door the very second she heard me putting my bike away. She had almost reached her yard by the time I saw her. Very quick. She must be in good shape from all those trips she's been making to the hospital."

"Dawn."

"Well, she makes me so mad! She sneaks around, visiting you and Gracie right under my nose, but she never visits me. And she never visits her mother either."

"She's dealing with things in her own way, Dawn."

"You mean she's avoiding things in her own way."

"Honey, this is an extremely difficult time for her. Her mother is not doing well. You know that."

"Yes, because I'm the one who visits her mother."

"But she's Sunny's mother, not yours, Dawn. We don't know how we'll react when we find ourselves in difficult situations. We always think we know, but we don't. Not really."

"But I'm in the same difficult situation she is."

"No, you're not. Because Mrs. Winslow isn't your mother."

I stared at Carol. And neither are you, I thought. For just one little teeny split second I hated Carol. Then the moment passed.

I shrugged and stood up from the table. I used to think of Carol as my wicked stepmother, but not anymore. She can still drive me crazy, but in a more normal way.

I changed the subject. "How are Gracie's teeth?"

"Coming in just fine." Carol grinned. "She'll be well armed when she reaches the biting stage." Carol put the empty bottles in the recycling can. Then she said, "Dawn, I am convinced that you and Sunny will be friends again one day. Just give her time."

Sunday night 2/7

I am bored.

What a rich and fulfilling weekend this has been. Baby-sitting (for three hours), one hospital visit, one bike ride, a few dull phone calls, playing Monopoly with Jeff, watching Gracie's teeth come in, homework. Yada, yada, yada. I am exhausted from all the excitement.

Later Sunday night 2/7

I heard somewhere that if you want excitement, you have to create it. Or maybe I made that up. Anyway, after letting boredom wash over me, I decided to un-bore myself.

First I called Maggie again. "Hey," I said.

"Hey," she replied.

"What are you doing?"

"Studying. History test tomorrow. First thing."

"Ugh."

I think Maggie wanted to get off the phone, but that would have made for a sad first attempt at un-boring myself, so I just asked point-blank. "How's your weight?"

Maggie was in a huge rush to get off the phone. "Fine. I gained two more pounds." She actually sounded proud of herself, which pleased me. I didn't think we would have to eat any more meals watching Maggie pick at a carrot shaving and then announce that she was full.

"Well . . ."

"Well, I really have to finish studying," said Maggie. (Very few things can come between Maggie and her studying.) "I'll see you tomorrow, okay?"

"Yeah. See you."

I put the phone down, then picked it up and called Ducky. "What are you doing?" I asked him.

"I just finished dinner."

I looked at my watch "Now?" It was a quarter to ten.

"Yeah. I thought my brother was coming home, but I guess he isn't. Not yet, anyway. So I finally took the pizza out of the oven. I ate all of it except for the two pieces I dropped on the floor. I saved those for Ted."

I laughed. Ducky didn't. I thought he sounded a little sad or something. "Ducky? Is everything okay?"

"Sure."

I knew it wasn't. I cast around for what could be wrong. Let's see. He was worried about Sunny. He missed his parents. Oh, wait. Alex. He missed Alex or felt guilty about him or was mad at him. "Is it Alex?" I asked.

Ducky was startled. "What?"

"Is that what you're upset about?"

"I didn't say I was upset."

"I know, but you are."

Ducky sighed. "I called his mother today. Alex probably isn't going to come back to Vista anytime soon."

"Really?"

"Yeah."

"Why not?"

"He just . . . isn't."

"But *why*?" I pressed.

"He needs special, um, treatment. For at least a few months. I guess he'll be in a hospital or something."

I didn't know what to say. I mean, he's Ducky's best friend and he tried to kill himself.

"Dawn?" said Ducky after a moment. "It's okay."

"I know. I know it will be, anyway. But it's awful right now."

"Yeah."

"What's the worst part?"

Ducky paused for so long that I said, "Is it that you miss him?"

"No."

"What, then?"

"That I think I could have prevented it from happening."

"Oh, Ducky. Don't do that to yourself. Anyway, you kept the <u>worst</u> from happening," I pointed out.

"Yeah." Ducky did not sound convinced.

I changed the subject. "Sunny came over today."

"You're kidding. Really?"

"To visit Carol. She fled when I came home."

"I'm glad she talks to Carol," said Ducky.

For some reason, tears sprang to my eyes. "Well . . ." was all I managed to say.

"Dawn, just go easy on her."

When Carol says things like that I want to stick my tongue out at her. When Ducky says them, I just love him even more.

"Okay," I replied.

Even later Sunday night 2/7

After I hung up the phone I was going to call Amalia, but the conversation with Ducky had tired me out. And then the phone rang and it was Amalia. Of course, when Carol called me to the phone she had to whisper, "Tell your friends not to call so late."

I looked at my watch again. It was 10:05. I couldn't decide whether that was actually late for a phone call, so I didn't say anything. I just took the phone from Carol.

"Hi, it's Amalia," said Amalia. "Is it too late to call?"

I considered. "Carol thinks so, but I don't," I said finally.

Amalia laughed. Then we talked about

school and Brendan and Maggie and Ducky and even Sunny (a little). Finally I noticed that Carol was standing in the kitchen doorway, circling her finger at me, which is her embarrassing way of silently telling me to wind up the call. I made a face, but when we reached a lull in the conversation, I said, "Amalia, I have to go." I was going to whisper that Carol was making me get off the phone, but she was still standing right there. Luckily Amalia understood.

"Yeah. My dad's telling me to go too. I'll see you in school tomorrow."

Study hall, Monday 2/8

Last night when I got off the phone I didn't go to sleep. I had created enough excitement with my phone calls so that I was just a little too keyed up to fall asleep. I found the newspaper and took it into bed with me. Not that dinky 8-page paper, but the

Palo City weekly paper. I thumbed through it. Headlines ran by my eyes. Stuff about the school board, potholes, the town's budget. Yawn, yawn, yawn.

Then I read the wedding announcements, the birth announcements, and the police blotter.

And _then_ a headline caught my eye that was so exciting it was responsible for keeping me up until nearly 3:00. It read: JAX TO PLAY IN NORTH PALO. Since I didn't believe this could actually refer to _the_ Jax, I almost turned the page. But something made me glance at the article anyway, and I nearly began screaming. I had to read the first paragraph twice to make sure I understood it. But sure enough, it said that Jax, "the rock phenomenon from Belgium," was going to play a concert — a single concert — at a club in North Palo in a few weeks.

Jax. The real Jax.

The band of my dreams.

The band for which Pierre X is one of the singers.

I know almost nothing about him except that I am in love with him.

I *have* to get to that concert.

Math class, Monday 2/8

Possible names X could stand for:

Xavier — is that a Belgian name? (Does it have to be a Belgian name? Maybe Pierre's family is from some other country.)

Xanadu. Well, you never know.

Xerxes. This is the dorkiest name in the history of the world, but there just aren't that many names that begin with X. I'm desperate. Anyway, maybe Pierre shortened his name precisely because it *is* dorky.

X-tremely Adorabl

Monday afternoon 2/8

I almost got caught, which would have been majorly humiliating. Amanda

Janson walked by my desk really s-l-o-w-l-y, and I realized that she had noticed I was writing in my journal. I guess she just _had_ to see _what_ I was writing about. (Clearly, Amanda does not yet understand the concept of our journals. Maybe she will after she's been at Vista a little longer.)

Anyway. Back to more important things.

I _HAVE_ TO GET A TICKET TO THE CONCERT.

Wednesday 2/10

Reasons I am in love with Pierre:

1. He is _so_ cool when he's onstage.

2. When he sings, he closes his eyes and you can just tell that he's lost in his own world, which must be a wonderful place.

3. I've never seen him in person, but I imagine that when he sings he gets a little bit sweaty. Not drippy sweaty, but just damply sweaty. So you

can just barely smell it, and it isn't a bad smell, but actually attractive. Like you'd sort of want to lean into him and collapse against his chest.

4. His hair curls at the nape of his neck.

5. When he gives interviews he looks RIGHT INTO the eyes of the interviewer. (If I were an interviewer, I would melt into a puddle.) And his eyes are piercing yet gentle. They are sincere eyes.

Thursday 2/11

Jax tickets go on sale on Monday. Numbered bracelets for the tickets will be given out on Saturday.

I HAVE TO GET A TICKET.

I HAVE TO SEE PIERRE LIVE, IN PERSON.

Later Thursday 2/11

Also, I <u>HAVE</u> to get to North Palo on Saturday so I can stand in that bracelet line. The bracelet line could be my only ticket to a ticket to seeing Pierre live.

Hmm. I will have to handle this subject carefully with Dad and Carol. I don't think they're going to want to drive me to North Palo to wait in an endless line. Of course, they are not going to want me to attend a late-night concert at a club in North Palo either, but I'll cross that bridge after I get a ticket. I think I'll call Maggie.

Thursday night 2/11

Maggie must be the only thirteen-year-old in the entire county who doesn't want to go to the Jax concert. It's really unfortunate, since I <u>know</u> her father would have provided his limo and driver to take us there.

This was my disappointing conversation with Maggie:

"Hi, it's me."

"Hey, Dawn."

"Hey. So . . . how many tickets are you going to try to get for Jax?"

"Jax?"

"The _group?_"

"What group?" Maggie is clueless.

"You know. Pierre? Pierre _X?_"

"Um . . ." Not a glimmer of recognition.

"Well. Then I guess you aren't going to be lining up for a bracelet."

"No . . . Should I?"

"I guess not. Not if you don't know Jax."

"I really don't."

"That's okay. They're kind of new."

After we hung up I had a brainstorm. Call _Amalia._ Much more sensible. I should have called her in the first place.

Later Thursday night 2/11

Not only is Amalia going to try to get tickets to Jax, but Isabel wants to go too, and some friend of Isabel's boyfriend is taking his van to North Palo first thing Saturday morning. There's room for me! Tomorrow at breakfast I'll ask Dad if I can go. I'll try to catch him when he's really busy — like feeding Gracie and reading the newspaper at the same time. When I mention it's a daytime trip and Amalia will be along too, I think he'll say okay.

Homeroom, Friday morning 2/12

It worked! Dad said yes! I can't wait to tell Amalia the news.

Friday afternoon 2/12

My plans for tomorrow:

1. Set alarm for 5:30. (Have I EVER gotten up at 5:30 on a Saturday?)

2. Hope to be out of bed by 6:00.

3. At 6:45, van will arrive.

4. Bracelets will be given out starting at ten, but we want to be in line EARLY just in case. This is our ONLY SHOT at tickets.

5. While we're waiting in line, one or two of us can leave and bring food back for the others.

MY FINGERS ARE CROSSED.

Friday night 2/12

A close call. A little while ago I was starting to get ready for bed when Dad knocked on my door.

"*Where* is it you're going tomorrow morning?" he asked.

"Um, to North Palo?"

"And this is for a concert?"

"Oh, no. It's just to see about some tickets," I said vaguely.

"Dad?" Jeff called from his room. "Can you help me?"

Perfect timing, little brother, I thought. Dad has not come back to my room. I think he's forgotten.

Saturday night 2/13

Whoa. What a day.

I managed to get out of the house before anyone else was actually up. I got nervous when I heard Gracie cry at five minutes to six, but Carol took her into bed with her and Dad, and they all went back to sleep. So no one else was up when I ran outside to get in the van. (I left a really bright and pleasant note on the kitchen table, saying I'd be back by the afternoon.)

Everyone in the van was sleepy but keyed up. Isabel and her friends were drinking coffee from a thermos. I cannot even pretend to like coffee. So I just pretended that I was older than thirteen. No one paid attention to Amalia and me, though. They left us alone in the backseat.

Guess what. We were not the first in line. About forty people were there ahead of us, camped out along the sidewalk. By ten, HUNDREDS of people were in the line behind us. Literally HUNDREDS. I was amazed. Amalia and I left our group a couple of times to buy juice and fruit and we kept bumping into people we knew. I saw kids I hadn't seen in years — kids who had lived on my street and moved away, kids who had transferred from Vista to other schools. I even saw our old baby-sitter Carl. I'll have to ask Jeff if he remembers Carl.

Anyway, right at ten o'clock, they began giving out bracelets. Amalia and I looked at the numbers on ours and shrugged.

"Well," said Amalia.

"Well," I said.

"We'll keep our fingers crossed."

We were home by 11:00.

Jeff doesn't remember Carl.

Later Saturday night 2/13

Waiting, waiting.

I just read in People that Pierre X witnessed a minor car accident in Malibu last week and he stopped to help the people in the cars. No one was too seriously hurt, but Pierre waited with them until the paramedics arrived. He handed out autographs before he left.

Pierre is so kind.

Even later Saturday night 2/13

I wonder if Pierre has a house in Malibu.

Maybe Amalia and I should try to get to Malibu someday. Is Pierre listed on a star map? (Try to find out.) He probably isn't, since his main residence is in London.

Sunday 2/14

VALENTINE'S DAY!!

I can't believe it. I've been so caught up with Jax and Pierre and tickets that I actually FORGOT it was Valentine's Day until I came down to breakfast this morning and found envelopes and little hearts all over the table. Carol had made the kitchen look very festive. She even bought presents for everyone. She gave me silver heart-shaped earrings and red heart-shaped soap. I'll have to make some Valentine's Day cards this afternoon. It's Gracie's first Valentine's Day.

Monday 2/15

Presidents' Day. No school.

Isabel and friends are driving back to North Palo this afternoon. Amalia and I will go with them. By tonight I'll know whether I'll get to see Pierre

LIVE. I only have enough money to buy 1 ticket, but that's all I need.

My fingers are permanently crossed.

Monday night 2/15

Desolation.

Amalia and I joined the crowd of people in North Palo again. We held our breath as a number was called out. It was 248. I didn't even need to look at the number on my bracelet. I already knew it was 681. There was no way I was going to be able to buy a ticket. People lined up according to their bracelet numbers, starting with 248. Each person could buy 1, 2, 3, or 4 tickets. The club seats 400 people.

Tickets were sold out by bracelet #507. Amalia and I tried not to cry on the way home.

Tuesday 2/16

Mrs. Winslow is home from the hospital! Carol just told me. I think I'll go visit her. (I know Sunny isn't there.)

Tuesday evening 2/16

I don't know why the doctors sent Mrs. Winslow home. She looks AWFUL. Maybe she just *wanted* to be at home. But still. Is it safe? What if something happens?

An aide was with Mrs. Winslow when I rang the bell. She was helping her take a shower. (Mrs. Winslow can't stand up for very long, so she sits on this special shower chair.)

I stayed with Mrs. Winslow for awhile after her shower. She is now completely bald. She didn't bother to wear a scarf or anything. At first. Then she got cold and put on a hat.

I came home and cried.

Thursday 2/18

Mrs. Winslow is BACK in the hospital. I guess she wasn't ready to come home after all.

Thursday night 2/18

Just when I was feeling my worst, really HORRIBLE, Ducky called.

OH! MY! GOD!!!

I CAN'T BELIEVE IT!

I haven't talked to Ducky in a few days, so I had no idea that he'd been in line for Jax tickets and <u>his</u> bracelet was #261. And so he scored FOUR TICKETS. Now get this. He just called and said he wants to take Amalia, Sunny, and me to the concert.

When Ducky told me this I screamed so loudly into the phone that I hurt his ear and he yelped. And Carol thought something had happened to me and came flying into the kitchen to see what was the matter. The moment she came flying in, I realized something. I couldn't tell her why I had screamed. Because I can't tell her about the concert. Not yet. I am going to have to approach the concert issue VERY carefully. Dad and Carol are not going to take well to the concert. I mean, I don't think that I can say to them, "Can Ducky drive Amalia and Sunny and me to North Palo late on a Friday night to go to a Jax concert in a club where liquor will be served?" and expect them to reply, "Oh, sure, honey. You go along. Have lots of fun."

Anyway, I'm off the subject.

I waved Carol out of the kitchen, saying, "Oh, Ducky just told me some good news. Sorry I scared you."

Then I apologized to Ducky for nearly destroying his hearing.

He said, "That's all right. I guess we should get used to it. The concert is going to be really loud. So anyway, this means you want to go?"

"Are you kidding me? Yes, *yes*,

YES!" I paused. "I hope Dad and Carol will <u>let</u> me go," I added.

"You think they might not?"

"I don't know. A late night. Drinking at the club."

"Hmm," said Ducky. "Well, talk to them, and let me know what happens, okay?"

"Sure. I may have to work on them slowly, though."

Friday 2/19

Of course, all I have been able to think about since last night is the concert. I AM REALLY AND TRULY GOING TO GET TO SEE PIERRE X!!!! I still can't quite believe it. Last night I actually pinched myself to make sure I wasn't dreaming. (I wasn't. And now I have a bruise on my thigh.)

I have been daydreaming endlessly about Pierre. It will be fantastic to see him in person . . . but what if, somehow, I get to MEET him? Maybe Ducky and

I could hang around the back entrance of the club and when the band members leave I could thrust a slip of paper at Pierre and he could AUTOGRAPH it for me. Maybe he would even write his full name and I would find out what the X is for.

No. I can't hang around and wait for his autograph like some silly Beatles fan. That's no good.

Maybe I could encourage Ducky to have a little car accident on the way home. Just a *slight* one. And then Pierre would happen along in his red Jaguar (I'm positive that's what he drives) and stop to help us. That way, not only would I get a personal greeting and an autograph, but I might even get to *touch* him.

Better yet

Oh, got to go. Dinner.

Late Friday night 2/19

I just thought of something. I have

been so wrapped up in the excitement of the tickets and my fantasies about Pierre that I've barely paid attention to one horrifying detail. Ducky said he wants to take Amalia, me, and SUNNY to the concert.

SUNNY.

An evening with SUNNY.

With SUNNY?

What was I thinking?

Saturday morning 2/20 9:02

I cannot go to the concert with Sunny. I just can't.

Saturday morning 2/20 9:07

Not see Jax live? Not see Pierre in person? I must be crazy. Of course I'm going to go to the concert.

Saturday morning 2/20 9:10

With <u>SUNNY</u>????

Saturday evening 2/20

I have been thinking about the Sunny dilemma all day. Obsessively. I've thought about it way more than about having to ask Dad and Carol for permission to go to the concert in the first place. Maybe I should worry about <u>that</u> instead. After all, the concert is in just 13 days. I have a lot of work to do.

Saturday night 2/20 10:42

13 NIGHTS FROM RIGHT NOW I WILL BE IN THE SAME ROOM WITH JAX AND PIERRE X!!!!!

Saturday night 2/20 10:44

If Dad and Carol let me go.

Sunday 2/21

All right. I decided I have to settle down and concentrate on how to handle the concert. I called Ducky.

"Hey, it's me," I said when he answered the phone.

"Hi, Dawn."

(I love when people recognize my voice and I don't have to say who I am. It's such a nice intimate feeling because it means you know somebody _really_ well. I think that voice recognition over the phone is an important step in a friendship.)

"How are you?" I asked.

"Good," replied Ducky, although he really didn't sound too good. "Did you talk to your parents about the concert yet?"

"No. I decided to talk to you first.

I'm pretty sure I can convince Dad and Carol to let me go. I just have to handle it carefully. But there's one other thing."

"Yes?" said Ducky patiently.

"Yes." I paused. "Sunny."

I think that a little teeny corner of me was hoping that Ducky would recognize my extreme discomfort at the thought of spending an evening with Sunny, and he would offer to (somehow) uninvite her. I held my breath.

"What about Sunny?" Ducky said.

"Well, we're still not speaking," I began, "and . . . we haven't exactly spent much time together lately."

"So you think the concert might be uncomfortable for you?"

"Yes!"

"Then maybe you should try to talk to Sunny before the concert."

"Oh."

"You should talk to her anyway, Dawn. I mean, you two should be friends again. You've been friends for such a long time. And if Sunny ever needed you, it's right now."

"Ha."

"No, really."

"Ducky, I love you. You know that. So pardon me when I say that you're such a <u>guy</u>. That is such a guy thing to say."

This was followed by a pause so long that I thought Ducky might have left the phone for some reason. Finally I said, "Ducky?"

After another slight pause he said, "Yeah. I'm here."

"What's the matter?"

"Nothing."

I frowned, which, of course, Ducky couldn't see.

A few minutes later we got off the phone.

School, Monday 2/22

Study hall. I just passed Sunny coming out of the library. I was about to say hi to her, but she didn't see me, and I didn't feel like calling out to her. I'm not sure why. I know that if she had looked up and seen me I would have said hi. But she didn't so I didn't. And now I feel small and mean, which is silly because she doesn't even know that I just walked by her.

Monday afternoon 2/22

Ducky dropped by after school today. Unannounced. (I think maybe he had gone to Sunny's house first, but she wasn't home, so he came over here.) It was unusually warm today, so we sat in the sun on our back steps. Carol wheeled Gracie out in her stroller and parked her in the shade. Ducky and I watched over her while she napped.

"Dawn?" said Ducky. "Do you think Maggie minds about the tickets?"

"What do you mean?"

"Well, you guys are all friends. You and Sunny and Amalia and Maggie. And me. And I gave tickets to everyone except Maggie."

"Well, you couldn't get more than four tickets. Maggie knows that. And she didn't want to go to the concert anyway. She doesn't even know who Jax is."

"You're kidding."

"Nope. She really doesn't."

"But do you think she feels left out anyway?"

"Ducky, you worry too much."

"I know."

Worrying is sort of Ducky's function in life.

After a moment Ducky said, "You didn't answer my question."

I sighed. "Well, I haven't spoken to Maggie about it, but I don't think you hurt her feelings. I really don't."

Ducky was certainly obsessing about Maggie, which gave me an idea. I remembered when I was obsessing about Groundhog Day. Maybe Ducky was actually worrying about something else.

"Are you thinking about Alex again?" I asked suddenly.

Ducky looked at me out of the corners of his eyes but didn't turn his head. "I think about him every day," he replied.

"Ducky, what Alex did was not your fault. It had nothing to do with you."

"How do you know?"

"He tried to kill himself. He tried to kill *himself*."

"But maybe I wasn't a good enough friend to him."

"Oh, that is so self-centered. Don't give yourself so much credit."

Ducky looked wounded, just for a moment. Then he burst out laughing. "I don't know whether to feel insulted or comforted," he said.

I laughed too. "Look, don't worry. Maggie is not going to kill herself because you didn't give her a ticket to a concert by a group she's never heard of."

Gracie started to fuss then, and Carol appeared at the back door, tugging at her blouse. Ducky leaped to his feet and announced that he had to leave. I couldn't blame him.

Monday night 2/22

Carol and I sat on the back steps while she fed Gracie.

"What do you think it means that Mrs. Winslow is already back in the hospital?" I asked.

"I think it means that it turned out to be more difficult to care for her at home than the Winslows had imagined," Carol replied. "Right now she needs so many procedures that are more easily done at the hospital." Carol shifted Gracie to her other breast.

I couldn't tell if Carol was telling the truth or not.

Either way I felt horrible for Sunny.

Tuesday night 2/23

I visited Mrs. Winslow at the hospital this afternoon.

Yikes.

This time she wasn't joking about pirates or hairstyles. All she did was lie in her bed. She could barely move. I saw that she didn't have the energy to move. I mean, she could barely raise an arm or turn her head. Her mouth is covered with sores from the chemo and they hurt her so much that she can't eat. The sores go all the way down her throat, I think. Even sipping water hurts her.

She looked SO ill that I thought she might not want me to stay. After all, she couldn't talk. So after I'd told her absolutely everything I could think of about school, my family, the concert (I even told her about being in love with Pierre X and I think she tried to smile), I stood up and said that maybe I better leave.

But that was when Mrs. Winslow did

manage to move a little. She put her hand on my arm. So I sat down again.

Now what?

What was left to talk about? I couldn't think of anything, so I reached into my backpack and pulled out <u>Franny and Zooey</u>, by J. D. Salinger. I'm really enjoying the book and I thought Mrs. Winslow might like to hear it, even if she'd already read it.

I read to her until Mr. Winslow appeared. Then I left.

Later Tuesday night 2/23

Things to tell Mrs. Winslow if she still can't talk the next time I visit her:

1. Jeff got an honorable mention in the science fair for his project, "The Food Chain."

2. Mary Anne <u>might</u> visit over spring break.

3. The plots of any movies I've seen lately.

4. What Carol tried to fix for dinner
5. (Nothing else is coming to mind.)

Wednesday afternoon 2/24

I popped into the hospital after school today. Mr. Winslow had been there at lunch, and two of Mrs. Winslow's friends were just leaving. I had been hoping for some miniscule improvement in Mrs. Winslow's condition. Truly. A _miniscule_ improvement would have been acceptable. But she seemed worse. She was just lying in bed with her eyes closed. I thought she was asleep. So I whispered to her friends, "I'll come back tomorrow."

But one of the friends said, "No, that's okay. She's awake." Then they left. I watched them hurry down the hall.

I fished around in my pocket for the list of things to tell Mrs. Winslow, glanced at it, and put it back. Nothing felt right.

Then I opened *Franny and Zooey* and continued reading.

Cafeteria, Thursday 2/25

Pouring rain today.

Ducky was just here. We split a juice.

I asked Ducky if he's visited Mrs. Winslow recently.

"I've only been to the hospital once," he said. "A couple of months ago."

I forget that Ducky hasn't known us very long. He seems like such an old, old friend.

"Oh. I went yesterday," I told him. "Ducky, she looks — HORRIBLE." (Ducky winced.) "Yeah. And each time I see her, she looks even worse, no matter how bad she already looked."

"Poor Sunny."

"Poor *Sunny*? What about poor Mrs. Winslow?"

"Dawn, how would you feel if Mrs. Winslow were *your* mother?"

I looked at the table. "Awful," I replied. "No. You know what? I don't even know how I'd feel."

I decided it was time to talk to Sunny.

Thursday afternoon 2/25

I visited Mrs. Winslow again after school. (I just read some more *Franny and Zooey* to her because she still can't talk.) When I was leaving, I ran into Sunny. I was zipping up my jacket as I stepped into the hallway, and I nearly bumped into her.

"Oh, sorry," I said. "Hi."

"Hi," replied Sunny, but she sounded as if she'd just seen a snake.

"I was visiting your mom."

Now, I know that was an unnecessary thing to say, but I don't think it deserved such a withering look from Sunny.

"No kidding," she said.

"Well, I think she likes the company."

Right away I knew I shouldn't have said that. I didn't mean to imply that Sunny should visit her mother more often, but that's how she took it.

"I'm sure she does, Pollyanna," replied Sunny.

I lowered my eyes and walked away.

Thursday night 2/25

I have been trying to tell myself that going to the concert with Sunny will be just fine. I think about the things Ducky has been saying. I think how horrible _I'd_ feel if _my_ mother were as sick as Sunny's. Plus, I remind myself of the years of friendship Sunny and I had before our fight.

Now, after our meeting at the hospital, I wonder if we can survive the concert together. Just thinking about it is making me squirm. And shiver.

Later Thursday night 2/25

Why does Sunny want to make people feel so miserable? What is she thinking?

Even later Thursday night 2/25

I just asked Carol my question about why Sunny would want to make people feel miserable. Carol said she doesn't think that's what Sunny is doing.

"But she was so mean to me today!" I exclaimed. "And she's been mean to a lot of people lately."

Carol drew in a breath. "How can I explain this?" she said. "Dawn, I think Sunny feels that if she isn't close to people, then if they leave her too, the way her mother seems to be leaving her now, it won't hurt so much."

"But I'm not leaving her!"

"I know. But I think Sunny thinks you *could* leave her. After all, anyone could get sick."

At first I just stared at Carol. How morbid. But then I understood what she was saying. "Or die in a car accident," I added.

"Or something less drastic," said Carol. "Move away. Switch to a different school. Sunny isn't taking any chances right now."

"But if she pushes everyone away from her," I went on, "maybe no one can leave her, but she won't have any friends either."

"I didn't say this was rational," Carol replied.

"Sunny needs a shrink."

"She probably does need to see a therapist," Carol said, "but that's up to Sunny and her parents."

Friday 2/26

A small daydream about Pierre and me:

Pierre and I somehow get to spend a weekend together. We can do absolutely anything we want to do. So what do we decide on? A nice, cozy weekend at home. We start off by grocery shopping. We buy everything we need to cook up a fancy meal. Roaming the vegetable aisle is SO romantic. Our hands touch as we both reach for the same clump of cilantro. We fill up our cart. Tomatoes, beans, garlic. Pierre says he knows how to make strawberry shortcake, so we buy two huge cartons of fat, scarlet strawberries.

On the way home from the grocery store, we stop at the video rental place. They're offering a special — three movies for three days for three bucks. So we choose _Gone With the Wind_, _When Harry Met Sally_, and _Buffy the Vampire Slayer_. We buy all-natural microwave popcorn and we're out of there.

We spend the entire afternoon cooking, in a very romantic way. When our supper is ready we decide to eat by candlelight — but we also want to eat by the fireplace in the living room _and_ in front of the TV in the den. So we decide to set a table in the living room, make a fire, and put candles on the table. When supper is over we move into the den and begin a movie marathon.

After the third movie, it is

Oh. It is time for class.

Cafeteria, Friday 2/26

I just caught sight of Sunny and I decided to be brave again.

"Hey, Sunny!" I called.

She turned around and saw me. "Yeah?"

A thousand thoughts swirled around in my head. I could ask her if she wants to go to the hospital together to visit her mother. (No, she would HATE that.) I could say, "Glad we're going to the concert." (Very lame.) I could invite her over. I could ask her if she wants to go shopping or something.

Finally I said, "Can I call you tonight?"

Sunny frowned slightly. "Uh, sure."

I felt like a dork. I watched Sunny walk out of the cafeteria. Where was she going? Our lunch period had just started. Clearly she wasn't sticking around for it.

Now I am sitting by myself with my uneaten lunch. I am going to look for Maggie and Amalia.

Later Friday 2/26

Well.

I can't believe what Maggie just told me. Sunny left lunch because she thought she could make it to the hospital for a quick visit with her mother and back to school, cutting only one class. (Why she can't go _after_ school is beyond me, but the important thing is that she's visiting her mother.)

Hmm.

Friday night 2/26 8:17

Okay. I am going to call Sunny like I said I would.

Friday night 2/26 8:18

Really. I'm going to call her.

Friday night 2/26 8:20

I'll call her as soon as I stop hyperventilating.

Friday night 2/26 8:23

Still catching my breath.

Oh god, there's the phone. Maybe it's Sunny.

Friday night 2/26 8:29

It was Ducky. He's so funny. He just called to say, "Can you believe that in a mere week we will be ON OUR WAY to see Pierre?"

I love that he's so excited. We chatted for a few minutes, but now I really HAVE to call Sunny. I mean, I told her I'd call her, so I better call her, right?

Okay. I am no longer hyperventilating. Now I will call her.

Friday night 2/26 8:30

She wasn't home.

Friday night 2/26 9:42

I just tried Sunny again and this time she answered the phone. I was finally — really and truly — ready to talk to her. To have a real talk. To try to sort out some of our problems before we get stuck sitting next to each other in the backseat of Ducky's car and then spending an entire evening together.

Here is our conversation:

Sunny: Hello?

Me: Hi, it's me.

Sunny: (Silence.) Um . . . who?

Me: Me, Dawn.

Sunny: (Totally flat voice.) Oh. Hi.

Me: (What I want to say is, "Calm down, you'll have a heart attack.") Uh, I said I'd call.

Sunny: (More silence.)

Me: Remember?

Sunny: Oh, yeah.

Me: Well, I was thinking we should talk.

Sunny: About what?

Me: About, you know . . .

Sunny: (More silence. She is not going to make this easy for me. Isn't going to help me out the least little bit. Once again, I do not say what I want to say, which is, "Sunny, for god's sake, you're my best friend. At least you used to be. We know each other better than anyone else does. At least we used to. Don't you want to be friends again? I miss you. And you need a best friend.")

Me: Sunny?

Sunny: Yeah?

Me: Don't you want to talk?

Sunny: Look, I'm kind of busy right now.

Me: (I think, Well, we can talk about that.) Oh? What are you doing?

Sunny: Just . . . stuff.

Me: (Sighing.) Sunny, don't you think we should at least talk before we go to see Jax?

Sunny: No.

Me: Okay, see you.

Sunny: 'Bye.

Friday night 2/26 9:50

I tried not to cry after I hung up the phone. I didn't want to give Sunny the satisfaction. But then I realized she'd never know if I cried, and anyway, I couldn't help it.

What is wrong with Sunny? Why doesn't she want to make up and be friends again? I'm trying to keep in mind the things Carol told me, but they aren't helping much.

Okay, Sunny. You've had your chance.

I think Ducky is going to have to separate us in the car. Put me next to him in the front and Sunny directly behind me so that we can't see each other. Then I'll play Ducky's tape player really loudly so nobody will be able to talk. (Often Ducky's tape player doesn't work, so maybe I'll bring a backup system.) I am not going to let Sunny ruin Pierre and the concert for me.

Saturday morning 2/27 9:22

I tried to forget about Sunny but she kept me up all last night. I could hardly sleep. I have an idea. I'll call

Ducky and suggest that somebody else drive Sunny to the concert.

What a good idea. I'll call him now.

Saturday morning 2/27 9:28

When I told Ducky my idea about sending Sunny in a separate car, he said, "Why would I do that?"

Good question. Hmmm. Why *would* he?

I had to come up with a stupid answer and then change the subject.

Saturday morning 2/27 9:31

It has just occurred to me that *I* don't even have permission to ride in Ducky's car. I still haven't talked to Dad and Carol about the concert.

Saturday night 2/27

I think I'll call Ducky again to

talk to him about Sunny and the concert. I don't think I introduced the subject in a well-thouht-out manner this morning.

Later Saturday night 2/27

Boy, does Ducky sound depressed. Really awful, actually. He was in such a good mood this morning, and tonight it's like I'm talking to a different person. (How do I wind up with all these moody people?)

Here is my conversation with Ducky:

Ducky: Hello?

Me: Hi!

Ducky: Hi, Dawn.

Me: What's going on?

Ducky: Not much. I just got home.

Me: (I look at my watch. It's, like, almost 10:00.) Yeah? Where were you? (I'm not nosy, just curious.)

Ducky: Out scoring dinner.

Me: What?

Ducky: There's no food in our

fridge. Well, practically none. Just condiments. And there was nothing in the freezer except ice. So I went out to get something to eat, but at each place I'd decide I didn't want the food there. So I drove around forever before I finally settled on fried rice.

Me: That was your entire dinner? Fried rice?

Ducky: Yeah. Nothing else appealed to me. I went to KFC first and decided I didn't want chicken. Then I went to Wendy's and decided I didn't want a hamburger. Then I went to Poppy's and decided I didn't want pizza.

Me: (All the time Ducky is talking I know I should be feeling sorry for him or something, but what I can't help thinking is how nice it must be to have your own car.)

Ducky: (Continuing.) Then I went to IHOP, but I didn't want pancakes. I was just about to give up and go home to eat mustard and ice cubes when I drove by the Lotus Garden and suddenly I decided I just had to have fried rice.

vegetable fried rice. So I got fried rice and a fortune cookie and came home.

Ducky was in such a weird mood. I couldn't tell whether this story was supposed to be funny or just sort of pitiful, so then I didn't know whether to laugh or make sympathetic noises. And *then* I didn't know whether to bring up the issue of Sunny. But I had to bring it up sometime. I couldn't keep *not* bringing it up or Sunny and I would end up together in the backseat of Ducky's car for sure.

Me: Ducky?

Ducky: Yeah?

Me: I really need to talk to you about something.

Ducky: (His mouth is full of either vegetable fried rice or the fortune cookie.) Okay. (He sounds uncertain.)

Me: Well, it's Sunny. And the concert.

Ducky: Dawn . . .

Me: But it's so uncomfortable being with her.

Ducky: Daw-*awn*. (Now he sounds annoyed.)

Me: But it *is*! Uncomfortable, I mean.

Ducky: Look, all you have to do is sit in the same car with her. The concert is going to be really crowded. You know that. You don't have to be anywhere near her if you don't want to be. They seat you at a table, but then you can get up and walk around. Okay?

Me: But she's so mean to me lately. (I know I sound like a baby. I can't help it.) I want to be friends with her, Ducky. I really do. I keep trying. I've tried talking to her. And she calls me Pollyanna or she won't talk to me at all. Why won't she make up with me?

Ducky: (He sounds softer now.) Dawn, I don't know. I'm glad you're trying, though. I want you guys to make up. I want all my friends to be happy. That's really important to me.

At this point, I keep my mouth shut for a moment. I know this is true.

After what happened to Alex, Ducky must be sort of desperate for all his friends to be happy. But that's a lot of pressure. I'm beginning to feel that I can't tell certain things to Ducky for fear of worrying him or at least disappointing him. My silence continues while I think all this stuff over.

Finally . . .

Ducky: You are going to come to the concert, aren't you?

Me: (First thinking about all the trouble Ducky went through to surprise us with the tickets and then imagining myself in the car with Sunny.) Oh, man . . . (Ducky is silent. I now imagine Pierre.) Of course I'm going to come to the concert. Are you sure Sunny can't ride in someone else's car?

Ducky: (Laughing.) Right. I'm going to drive to your house, pick you up, wave to Sunny next door, and call, "Your ride's on the way. Sorry you can't come with us, even though we have room, but I wanted to work out something more complicated. See you at the concert."

Me: (Now I'm laughing.) Okay, okay. I'll be big about this.

Ducky: Great.

Me: Now I just have to convince Dad and Carol to let me go.

Ducky: <u>What?</u> You still haven't gotten permission?

Me: Not exactly. I mean, no.

Ducky: And you put me through all this when you don't even know if you'll be coming with us?

Me: Oh, I know I'll be able to come. I just have to do a little planning.

Ducky: You have less than a week.

Me: That's plenty of time.

Ducky: I hope so.

Me: 'Night, Ducky. I'll see you on Monday.

Ducky: 'Night, Dawn.

Sunday morning 2/28

I feel that I've been a little too good lately. I need to do something daring. Or at least fun. Hmm. I think I'll call Maggie.

Sunday night 2/28

Maggie and I spent the day together. Maggie is SO much more fun now that she's eating again. Before it was always, like, "Oh, no, I can't eat that." Or, "Oh, no, I can't eat dinner." She might as well have added, "Are you crazy? I just ate dinner last week." Which, horrifyingly, was sometimes practically the truth. She was no fun shopping or at a party. Even at school when she started skipping lunch and she wasn't even IN the cafeteria, Amalia and I found ourselves sitting around discussing Maggie's absence and what it could mean. We were <u>always</u> discussing Maggie and her weight and her appearance and the horrible tiny meals she'd eat, when she ate at all.

But now that Maggie's getting some help, she's eating again. And she's not so obsessed with food. We can go to a restaurant and she can order like a normal person instead of discarding absolutely every item on the menu because it has too many calories and then ordering a small bowl of lettuce leaves or something.

Anyway, I called Maggie and she said she didn't have any plans today, so we asked her dad's chauffeur to drop us off at Harmon's. We sauntered in there like we were going to look around that department store forever, but the second her car had disappeared we ran down the street and soon we were headed toward the Square. Dad and Carol can't stand the Square. They think the kids who hang out there are Trouble, like the ones in the "River City" song in The Music Man. Dad calls them punks and constantly reminds me of the dangers of marijuana. Ha. If only he knew what those kids really do. But Maggie and I weren't going to hang with the kids. We were more interested in the stores on the streets around the Square. You can get anything in them — leather clothes, ripped clothes, incense, hair dye. And you can get any part of your body pierced.

Maggie and I poked around and bought incense, and I bought an incense holder. Then I considered dyeing my hair black, but Maggie talked me out of it. Finally we went into this little restaurant, the one called the Tea Shop. You can buy an awful lot more than tea there, and I don't mean just food.

Later Sunday night 2/28

My hand was about to fall off. I had to stop writing for awhile.

Maggie and I didn't go into the back of the Tea Shop, which is where the interesting things happen. We sat at a booth by the front window. I ordered a veggie burger and Maggie ordered a salad — but a good, big, healthy salad with cheese and olives and stuff in it in addition to the vegetables. She even put some dressing on the salad and she ate almost the whole thing.

While we were eating I said, "I have to find a way to make Dad and Carol let me go to the concert next weekend."

"They won't let you go?"

"No, they haven't said that yet. But they're going to when they realize that the concert is in a club and that liquor will be served and that Ducky is driving us and it'll be late at night."

Maggie made a face. "Yikes," she said.

"I know."

"I'll help you. I'm good at this sort of thing."

"I know that too."

"Okay. First of all, be as honest as you can without telling the whole truth. That way, your dad and Carol can never say that you kept anything from them . . . exactly."

"For instance?"

"For instance, tell them the concert is going to be held in a club, not at a concert hall, and that ordinarily you'd get carded before you go in, but that this concert is open to all ages. They *should* figure out the liquor thing."

"Somewhere, in the backs of their minds," I added.

"Right. And later, if it's an issue, you can say, 'But I *told* you it was going to be held at a club.'"

"Okay."

"Then, of course, there's always begging, wheedling, promising, bribing, and bargaining." (I grinned.) "Although you don't have to try them in that order, and you have to be subtle about some of them." Maggie swallowed a radish and smiled at me.

The waitress (crew cut, green streak on top of head, two nose rings, five earrings in one ear, other ear naked, leather tank top, miniskirt) asked us if we wanted anything else. Maggie and I ordered tea so we could sit and talk a bit longer.

We made a list of how I could approach the concert with Dad and Carol. Here's the list:

1. Tell them about the concert and how badly I want to go. Don't tell them _everything_, but don't lie either. Impress upon them how much trouble Ducky went to in order to get the tickets.

2. If they say no, try begging.

3. If they still say no, try wheedling.

4. If they still say no, start making promises. (Like, I promise to wear my seat belt, to make Ducky stick to the speed limit, and to call the moment we get to the concert.)

5. If they are uncertain, try bribing them. Tell them which chores I'll do if they let me go.

6. As a last resort, try bargaining, but I may have to compromise the evening if I do.

Maggie and I hung out at the Square until 15 minutes before we were going to be picked up. Then we raced back to Harmon's. When the limo arrived, we were standing in front of the store looking exhausted from window shopping. (We had put our bags containing the incense and stuff into old Harmon's shopping bags that we'd hidden in our purses before we left.)

I plan to try #1 on the list tomorrow at dinner.

Monday night 3/1

Here is our conversation from dinner (clearly I am going to have to move on to #2 on the list, probably later tonight):

Dad, Carol, Jeff, and I sit down at the table. Gracie has just had a big snack of milk and is crawling around on the floor where we can keep an eye on her.

Dad: So, did everybody have a good day?

Jeff, me, Carol: Oh, yes, sure, yup.

Jeff: My math teacher is a bonehead.

Me: He is? Why?

Carol: It isn't nice to call people boneheads.

Jeff: Even if they *are* boneheads?

Dad: This salad is deLIcious.

Carol: Hearts of palm.

Me: I have some news. (Everyone looks at me.) It's . . . well, it's really fanTAStic! I am so excited!

Jeff: What is it? What is it?

Me: Ducky invited me to the Jax concert. Actually, he invited Amalia and Sunny and me. He got four tickets. Isn't that cool?

Jeff: (Nearly falling off his chair.) You're going to the JAX concert? Whoa. Oh, man, you are SO lucky! The Jax concert. Man . . . man . . . I didn't really think you'd get to go.

Dad: When and where is the concert?

Me: This Friday night. In North Palo.

Dad: How are you going to get there?

Me: Ducky's driving.

Carol: What time is the concert?

Me: Jax comes on at about eleven,

but the warm-up act starts earlier. Around ten, I think.

Dad: (Choking a little.) So you won't even be leaving here until nine or so? (He glances across the table at Carol and they exchange a meaningful look.)

Me: I don't know _exactly_ what time we'll be leaving, but yeah, probably around nine. Maybe earlier if we go out to eat first. (This has never been discussed, but I add it brightly because it sounds good.)

Dad: Carol and I will have to talk this over.

Later Monday night 3/1

After this disappointing dinner I called Maggie.

"Okay. On to number two," she said matter-of-factly.

"Yeah. That's what I thought."

I got my chance less than an hour after dinner. Dad and Carol were in the living room playing with Gracie, and Jeff was doing his math homework.

(I'm not sure, because I didn't ask, but I think the math teacher is a bonehead because of the length of this particular homework assignment.)

Anyway, it was a nice, quiet moment, so I took it as an opportunity to try begging. Also, to drive home the point about Ducky.

"Dad, Carol," I began, "Ducky went to a lot of trouble to get these tickets. And we didn't <u>ask</u> him to get them for us. It was, like, a surprise. He wanted to surprise us. It means a lot to him. To be able to take us, I mean. He wanted to treat us. You know what a hard time he's been through. Alex and everything. I don't want to hurt his feelings."

Carol nodded sympathetically. But Dad said, "I understand all that, Dawn. But we can't make decisions based on your friends' situations."

Since this did not sound very promising, I decided to move right to #3, wheedling, before Dad could even continue.

"Dad," I said, "I consider you and

Carol very enlightened parents." (I know Carol loves it when I refer to her as a parent rather than as a stepparent.) "And," I went on, ignoring the fact that Dad was clearing his throat and trying not to look at Carol, "I know you won't be swayed by the fact that the Winslows are letting Sunny go and Amalia's parents are letting her go. I know you'll just stick to the facts. And at least take Ducky's desperate situation into consideration. He's . . . vulnerable right now. But he's also an excellent driver. And the most responsible sixteen-year-old I know. Just very needy. He needs his friends. And I know how you two feel about being loyal to friends. It's practically a family value."

I paused to see what sort of reaction I was getting. It was interesting. Dad and Carol didn't say no. But they didn't say yes. I think I'll wait for them to make the next move. If they don't make it by tomorrow night, though, I'll move on to #4.

Cafeteria, Tuesday 3/2

I forgot to mention yesterday that Sunny's mom came home from the hospital again. When I returned from school an ambulance was in the Winslows' driveway. At first I panicked. I ran inside, calling for Carol. She and Gracie were out, but Mrs. Bruen was there, which was just as good. (Mrs. Bruen is like another mother to me.)

"Mrs. Bruen!" I cried. "There's an ambulance next door!"

Mrs. Bruen looked up from the pasta she was fixing for our dinner. "It's okay, Dawn," she said. "Mrs. Winslow just came home."

"In an ambulance? She had to ride in an ambulance?" This seemed very odd. If she was sick enough to need an ambulance, why was the hospital letting her go?

Mrs. Bruen nodded. "She's pretty sick, honey."

"I know, but . . ."

"I think she just wanted to come home."

"Maybe I'll go visit her."

"Why don't you wait a bit. Let her get settled first. It takes more time now. At least wait until the ambulance leaves."

I was so shaken by the sight of the ambulance that after awhile I decided not to visit her. Maybe I'll go this afternoon.

Tuesday afternoon 3/2

I am sitting at my desk, looking out my bedroom window. I can see the Winslows' driveway. In it is a delivery truck with the words HERITAGE SURGICAL on the side. Below is a list of some of the stuff that I guess this place either sells or rents to people: commodes, walkers, back and knee braces, bedsore products, hospital beds, ostomy supplies (whatever they are). The list goes on. Under the list, in larger letters, are the words ALL SICKROOM SUPPLIES.

I shivered when I read that last part. All sickroom supplies. It sounds so sad and sort of tragic.

This guy has been going in and out the Winslows' front door, carrying large cartons.

Hmm. What's going on? I was planning to visit Mrs. Winslow, but I guess I'll put it off again. At least until things seem quieter next door.

Tuesday afternoon 3/2

The truck left. I was just about to go next door when a car pulled into the Winslows' driveway and an older woman with curly graying hair stepped out carrying a bag. I know who she is. I've seen her before. I can't remember her name, but I recognize her. She's a visiting nurse. She comes by to do things like take blood samples and check blood pressure. Well. Now is not the time for a visit either.

Almost dinnertime, Tuesday 3/2

I was just about to go to the Winslows' once again — when Sunny came home. Won't go now. Maybe tomorrow.

Tuesday night 3/2

Dad and Carol didn't say anything about the concert at dinnertime. Which is why I had to bring it up myself later. This time I waited until both Gracie and Jeff were in bed.

"So," I said. "Have you had a chance to think about the concert?"

"Yes," Dad replied, "but we haven't reached a decision."

"The concert's on Friday!" I exclaimed. "That's in just three days." I sounded slightly hysterical so I calmed down. Then I hit on a tactic that would, if nothing else, force Dad and Carol to make a decision quickly. "If I can't go to the concert, I should let Ducky know right away so he can find someone else to give the ticket to." The truth is, I have absolutely no intention of not going to the concert. If Dad and Carol say I can't go, I'll have to sneak out. Or tell them I'm spending the night at Maggie's or something. But that's a last resort.

"Hmm, yes, I suppose you're right," said Dad.

"So can I go?" I asked.

Dad frowned. "It's the business of your being driven around so late at night by a sixteen-year-old," he began.

Even though Dad still hadn't said no, I jumped to #4 and began making promises. "But Ducky is an excellent driver, I promise!" I exclaimed. "And I promise I'll wear my seat belt. And I promise that Ducky never drinks and drives."

"I hope not," said Carol. "In any case, he's too young to drink."

"And I promise I'll keep everyone in the car really quiet," I went on. "Ducky won't have any distractions. And I'll make him stick to the speed limit. Which he does by himself anyway," I added hastily. "And I promise I'll call you the second we get to the club. I'll call later when we're leaving if you want. So you'll know when we're on our way home."

"Well," said Dad.

"Well," said Carol.

They were definitely uncertain, so I moved on to #5, hoping I wasn't overdoing things. "If you let me go, I'll clean out the garage."

Dad looked at me and started to laugh. So did Carol. "Okay, you can go," said Dad.

"Really?" I cried. "Really?"

"Really," said Dad and Carol.

"Thanks! Thanks!"

I ran across the room and hugged Dad first, then Carol.

"You drive a hard bargain," said Dad.

"Did I go overboard?"

"Maybe just a little."

"Do I really have to clean out the garage?"

"Yes."

Later Tuesday night 3/2

I won't mind cleaning out the garage. I can daydream about Pierre while I work. With any luck I'll have something real to daydream about.

Wednesday afternoon 3/3

When I got home from school today only one vehicle was parked in the Winslows' driveway. I didn't recognize it, but I decided to try visiting Mrs. Winslow anyway.

It turned out that the car belonged to a very nice woman named Simone, who called herself a home-health-care worker. As far as I can tell, her job is to help out around the Winslows' house (in particular, to fix meals), to keep Mrs. Winslow company when she's there alone, and to help her with things like bathing, changing her nightgown, and going to the bathroom. I liked Simone, BUT . . .

I couldn't believe it. Mrs. Winslow wasn't in her bed on the second floor. Instead, the dining room has been turned into her bedroom (I don't know where the table and chairs were moved to), and she's in an actual hospital bed. In fact, the room looks like a hospital room, with all sorts of equipment in it. The gross part? It SMELLS like a hospital room too. I can't pinpoint that smell, but it's kind of disgusting. It's medicine and pee and sweaty sheets and I don't know what else.

Ugh.

Mrs. Winslow seemed glad to see me. And she seemed better than she had been in the hospital. She could talk a bit because her mouth sores were getting better. She wasn't so sleepy either.

I sat in a chair next to her bed. I was holding _Franny and Zooey_, just in case. But we didn't need it. We could talk.

Well, we _tried_ to talk. But we were interrupted about a thousand times. Simone had questions about dinner, which she was preparing. So she kept poking her head through the doorway between the kitchen and the dining room, asking about Mrs. Winslow's appetite or where the spices were stored or what time Sunny would be home. Then I was right in the middle of telling how I had to clean the garage when the doorbell rang and in walked the visiting nurse.

I told Mrs. Winslow I'd come back the next day.

Thursday morning 3/4

TOMORROW NIGHT I WILL SEE PIERRE LIVE!!!

Countdown: 40 hours (approximately)

Thursday afternoon 3/4

Visited Mrs. Winslow as soon as I got home from school. Simone was there. Mrs. Winslow seemed a teeny bit better than yesterday and I was encouraged. She can talk even more, and now that she can talk, her sense of humor is back. She was making jokes about the fuzz that will soon start to grow on her head. It will probably be blonde, and Mrs. Winslow was saying she'll look like a chick.

"I always wanted to look like a cute chick," she said, "but I meant a cute chick, not a blonde chicken."

Mr. Winslow came home from work early. Simone showed him what she'd prepared for dinner and then she left. I started to leave too. I thought Mr. and Mrs. Winslow might want some time alone together, especially since they kept glancing at each other. So I stood up to leave, but Mr. Winslow said, "No, wait, Dawn. There's something we'd like to tell you. Sunny already knows and it's no secret anymore." He glanced at Mrs. Winslow again.

My heart leaped. Maybe Mrs. Winslow was in remission! Maybe they'd found a way to beat her cancer.

"Dawn," Mr. Winslow went on, "we've decided to terminate chemotherapy."

"Terminate it? You mean it's over? That's gr—"

Mr. Winslow held up his hand to stop me. "It's being terminated because it isn't working any longer. It's doing more harm than good."

I frowned, taking this in. Finally I said, "Well, what are they going to do instead? Radiation?"

Mrs. Winslow shook her head.

At this particular moment, Sunny walked through the front door. She saw me in the dining room with her parents, turned, and headed up the stairs to her room.

"Maybe I'll go talk to Sunny," I said to the Winslows.

They nodded.

At the bottom of the stairs I looked

up and saw Sunny sitting on the top step. She wasn't in her room after all.

"Hi," I said. "Your dad just told me —"

"I know what he just told you," Sunny said, interrupting.

"Well, do you —"

"No, I do not want to talk about it."

"But —"

"I SAID I do not want to talk about it."

I called good-bye to Mr. and Mrs. Winslow and left.

Later Thursday afternoon 3/4

I have to say that I'm kind of glad Carol took off so much time from work after Gracie was born. She's not going to go back for two or three more months, and I confess that (usually) I like finding her at home in the afternoons. Today was one of those days.

When I left Sunny's house I burst

through our front door and told Carol the Winslows' news.

Carol frowned. "Oh boy," she said softly.

"Do you think this means there's nothing left to do for Mrs. Winslow?" I asked. "We didn't really finish our conversation."

"I don't know."

Good old Carol. I might just have worried and wondered, but Carol phoned next door and talked to Mr. Winslow. When she hung up the phone she held her arms out and gave me a hug. Then she said, "No more treatment, Dawn. They've done everything they can do."

"But — but —" I sputtered. "But that's not fair! How can the doctors just *decide* something like that? It's Mrs. Winslow's life, not theirs. If the Winslows want to keep paying for treatments, then the doctors have to go along with that. Don't they?" I cried.

"Honey, it wasn't the doctors' decision."

"You mean it was Mr. Winslow's? But that's not fair either!"

"No, it was Mr. and *Mrs.* Winslow's decision, Dawn."

I was speechless. Carol sat me at the kitchen table and put the kettle on for tea. Then she sat down next to me.

Finally I said, "But why would Mrs. Winslow decide something like that? I don't understand."

"I think she's being realistic. The treatments aren't working. They aren't doing anything but making her sick."

"So no one's going to do anything for her anymore?"

"Oh, no. That's not what I mean," said Carol. "Mrs. Winslow will still be cared for. The doctors will do everything they can to make her feel as comfortable as possible. But they don't believe they can cure the cancer now."

Thursday night 3/4

I do not know what to think about Mrs. Winslow.

Friday morning 3/5

Tonight I am going to see Pierre live and in person. I wish I were as excited now as I was yesterday morning. But I can't stop thinking about Mrs. Winslow and

Uh-oh

Cafeteria, Friday 3/5

I stopped writing when I noticed an ambulance in the Winslows' driveway again. This time it was taking Mrs. Winslow back to the hospital. Something to do with her breathing.

Friday afternoon 3/5

I have to stop obsessing about Mrs. Winslow. It's making me crazy. I think I'll concentrate on the concert instead, which will take place in a mere seven (that's 7) hours. At that time I will see Pierre X. It is possible that I could be just a few yards away from him. A few YARDS.

Later Friday afternoon 3/5

Conversation with Dad the SECOND he got home from work:

Dad: So, are you excited about the concert, Dawn?

Me: I can't wait! Thanks again for letting me go with Ducky.

Dad: That's what I wanted to talk to you about.

Me: What.

Dad: About your driving to North Palo with . . . What is his real name, Dawn? It can't possibly be Ducky.

Me: (My stomach is clenching because maybe Dad has changed his mind.) No, it's Christopher. McCrae.

Dad: With Christopher. Dawn, I want you to promise me several things.

Me: (I am breathing an enormous sigh of relief.) Oh. Okay. (The truth is, I would promise just about anything right now, but I do not want to divulge this.)

Dad: Number one, Christopher will be —

Me: (I can't help interrupting him.) Dad, his name is Ducky. Absolutely no one ever calls him Christopher. Even our teachers. (This was not entirely true, but I didn't care.)

Dad: Okay, _Ducky_ will be the only driver.

Me: The rest of us are only thirteen, Dad.

Dad: But you never know who you might run into. And I do not want ANYONE else driving.

Me: Okay.

Dad: You wear your seat belt at all times.

Me: (I almost say, "Even during the concert?" but I think better of it.) Okay.

Dad: If Ducky does anything, and I mean ANYTHING at all, that makes you feel uncomfortable with his driving, you get out of the car and you call me.

Me: (I don't see how I would do that on the freeway, but . . .) Okay.

Dad: As you suggested, the moment you arrive at the club you call home to let Carol and me know you got there safely. And later you call us when you're leaving.

Me: Even if it's one o'clock in the morning?

Dad: No matter what time it is.

Me: Okay. I promise.

Friday evening 3/5 7:35

I have been standing in front of my

closet for 10 whole minutes and I have not found a single outfit that will be cool enough to wear to the concert.

I must make the right impression on Pierre.

Friday evening 3/5 7:54

Well. I suppose I have done my best. What I <u>wanted</u> to wear was an outfit like the one our waitress had on in the Tea Shop at the Square. But I wouldn't be allowed out of the house in it, which would sort of defeat the purpose. So I have settled on a vest over a white T-shirt with a black miniskirt. Dad has seen the skirt before, and while he doesn't actually approve of it, he doesn't disapprove of it either. The vest is just plain black cotton, but I'm hoping that if the club is dark enough it might be mistaken for leather. Surprisingly, my feet are dressed better than the rest of me. They are clad in my black high-heeled sneakers with the three-inch soles. I will be the tallest person in our group. Again, Dad does not like these shoes, but here's the great thing: Carol does. So there isn't much Dad can say about them.

I put on a nice tasteful pair of earrings. Then I tossed a really funky pair in my purse. I'll switch earrings in the car. That's okay. I have done this in the dark before.

Friday evening 3/5 9:02

Ducky will be here ANY MINUTE!!!!!

Friday evening 3/5 9:14

HE'S HERE!!!!!!!!!!

Saturday morning 3/6

I thought that when I sat down to write about last night and the concert and Pierre I would just scribble blissfully for a page or two. I didn't realize I would have such a story to tell.

But I do.

And it's going to take awhile to tell it.

Here goes.

I'd been watching out my window for Ducky's car. I saw it pull up to the curb between Sunny's house and mine. Even before I could turn away from the window, Sunny was flying through her front door and across the lawn to the car. (I tried to see what she was wearing, but it was too dark.) The car pulled into our driveway.

I ran out of my room, down the hallway, and into the living room.

"Ducky's here," I announced. I tried to sound formal and staid. I thought if I sounded too excited I would somehow also sound irresponsible. I stood before Dad and Carol in my outfit.

"Well. Don't you look, um . . ." said Dad.

"Don't you look ready for a concert!" said Carol brightly.

The doorbell rang. (I had told Ducky that Dad would want to talk to him.) Dad and I answered it together. I stood on the front stoop, chewing my lip, while Dad ran through all my "rules" with Ducky and then quizzed him on what he would do in certain emergency situations.

Ducky passed the test and we were allowed to go to the car. To my dismay I saw that Sunny was sitting in the front seat, which meant that she could control Ducky's radio (if it worked). I had decided not to bring a backup sound system, but I <u>was</u> counting on being in charge of the radio. Oh, well. I sat directly behind Sunny, where it would be harder for her to see me. It didn't matter. She swiveled her head around like an owl and greeted me with, "Did your Dad have a nice talk with Ducky?" (I could hear the smirk on her face.)

Before I could answer, Ducky swung himself into the driver's seat and punched a button on the tape deck. Music blared.

"Careful, Ducky," said Sunny. "Dawn's father might hear that and make her stay home."

Ducky reached under his seat and produced a baseball cap, which he clapped on his head with the bill facing directly to one side. "Mr. Schafer has no power here," he said to Sunny in an accented voice. "So becalm your fears."

I couldn't help laughing. "Becalm?" I said. "Is that a real word?"

"On my planet it is," Ducky replied.

We picked up Amalia without incident and were on our way.

"Now, this is nice," said Ducky as we edged onto the freeway a few minutes later. "Just me and my girls."

He was smiling the loveliest, happiest, most genuine smile.

Sunny turned to Ducky and flashed him an equally lovely smile. I realized that the evening must have been as important to her as it was to me, but for different reasons.

We made it to the concert without a single cross word between Sunny and me. This was because we didn't talk to each other at all, but that was fine. Ducky parked his car and we walked toward the club.

My funky earrings were in place. I was ready to go.

Saturday afternoon 3/6

A huge long line of people stretched out the entrance to the club and along the sidewalk. Each one looked cooler than the next. And I would have to say that the average age was about 20.

I was SOOOO glad my father couldn't see this.

"Do you have the tickets?" I asked Ducky.

"You think he has no brain, don't you," said Sunny. A statement.

"Yes, I have the tickets." Ducky shot Sunny a LOOK.

I ignored her.

We joined the line, which crept along, snail-like. When at last we reached the door, one person collected our tickets while another guy held out his hand and said, "ID?"

My heart leaped right into my mouth. I turned wildly to Amalia. "We need an ID to get in?" I whispered loudly.

Sunny heard me and snorted. "Not to get in," she said witheringly. "It's because they serve liquor here. If you have an ID, which means you're old enough to drink, then they give you a bracelet, and inside, the bartenders will only sell liquor to people wearing bracelets."

"Oh," I said, feeling foolish. But I frowned. The system seemed flawed to me, and sure enough, the moment we were inside, Sunny looked around and said, "Now, who can I buy a bracelet from?"

While Sunny was looking for a bracelet, I was looking for a pay phone. "I have to call my father," I reminded Ducky.

He helped me find a phone, I called Dad, and then we rejoined Amalia and Sunny (who was still not wearing a bracelet).

"Did your daddy say you could stay awhile longer?" Sunny greeted me. "Or did he decide he'd better come and get you?"

I smiled sweetly at her. "Oh, Sunny," I said. "I'm so sorry."

She looked at me sharply. "About what?"

"About your father. That he's so wrapped up in your mother that he doesn't care what you do."

Sunny had opened her mouth to say something, and Amalia and Ducky were just staring at me, when we were interrupted by this guy who turned out to be a friend of Ducky's brother.

"Hey! The Duck Man!" He clapped Ducky on the shoulder.

"Hi, Rick," Ducky replied unenthusiastically.

Sunny's eyes headed straight for Rick's wrist — which sure enough sported a plastic bracelet.

Before Sunny could ask about buying the bracelet, Rick asked, "Can I get you guys anything to drink?"

"Oh . . . no," I replied. "Thanks."

"Come on," said Rick. "Just a little something to help you relax and enjoy the show. Don't be shy."

I wasn't being shy. I was picturing my father, who, I was sure, would be waiting at the door when I came home. I didn't want him to know <u>any</u> of us had been drinking. Then it occurred to me that he'd probably only see Ducky and me. I didn't have to worry about what Sunny and Amalia did.

"Just a Coke for me," said Amalia.

"Me too," said Ducky.

"Seltzer for me," I said.

"Well, I'd like a rum and Coke," said Sunny.

"One rum and Coke, two plain Cokes, and a seltzer? Come on, live a little. Ducky, my main man, let me get you something stronger."

"Yeah, Ducky, go ahead. Friends don't let friends drink alone," said Sunny.

"Well . . ." Ducky was hesitating, looking interested now.

I cringed and glanced at my watch, trying to calculate how long before we were in the car again and whether Ducky would be in any condition to drive then if he had a drink now. I watched Ducky's face. I could almost see him thinking over the turmoil of the past weeks — Alex, Sunny, Sunny's mother . . .

"Well," said Ducky again, "sure. I'll have something. Just to relax. How about a —"

Rick didn't let him finish. "I'll be right back," he said.

Rick disappeared into the crowd. We still hadn't found our seats, and now we had to stay where we were until Rick came back. I peered around. We were standing in a busy hallway. Two bars were set up in it, one at either end. Between the bars was a set of double doors leading into a much larger room. I stood on tiptoe and tried to see into the room, which was dark and smoky. The room was jam-packed with tables and chairs, and at the far end was a stage. I closed my eyes. Soon I would be in there, gazing at Pierre on the stage.

Later Saturday afternoon 3/6

I had to give my wrist a rest before I continued. Also, Amalia just called to find out how much trouble I'm in. I was glad to hear from her. Since I'm grounded, I can't make any phone calls. I'm surprised Carol let me talk to her, since I'm not allowed to *take* calls from my friends either. Amalia must have been pretty persuasive. (She's good with adults.) Anyway . . .

Soon Rick came back with five drinks on a tray. He handed the tray to Ducky, removed one of the drinks, accepted some cash from Ducky, and walked off, calling, "Later!" over his shoulder.

I looked at the plastic glasses on the tray. One was a Coke and one was a bubbly seltzer (I hoped); two were clear liquid and smelled very strong.

"Hey, I said I wanted a rum and Coke," Sunny complained. But she reached for one of the glasses of clear liquid and sipped it anyway. "Not bad," she said.

Gingerly, I reached for the seltzer. I smelled it before I sipped it. The truth? I would kind of like to have had a *little* something to drink, like I did at the fateful party at Ms. Krueger's house, but I knew that if Dad so much as suspected I'd been drinking I'd be grounded until I was 30. My seltzer just smelled like seltzer, though, and tasted like it too.

I watched Sunny and Ducky to see how quickly they drank their drinks, whatever they were, and was pleased that they just sipped at them like Amalia and I were doing.

"Okay," said Ducky, "let's find our seats."

At long last we entered the big room with the stage. A girl wearing a Jax T-shirt showed us to a long narrow table, which seated twelve people. She indicated four seats at one end and we sorted ourselves out. Sunny and Ducky sat next to each other, and Amalia and I sat across from them.

I tried not to look at Sunny. Instead, I looked around the room, mentally rating people's outfits. No one rated lower than "extremely cool," except possibly me.

Ten minutes went by, and Rick and a girl with a shaved head materialized next to us.

"How are the drinks holding up?"

asked Rick. The girl looped her arm through his. Possessively, I thought.

"Oh, just fine," I said quickly. "No problem."

But Sunny's glass was empty except for the ice. "All gone!" she said, holding it up. She smiled.

Rick smiled back at her. "What'll it be, then?"

"Mm, how about a tequila sunrise this time?" Sunny paused, then she said, "No wait. Hold the sunrise."

"A shot of tequila?" said Rick, and he arched an eyebrow ever so slightly.

"Perfect," said Sunny.

"Duck Man?" asked Rick. "Are you relaxed yet?"

Ducky's glass wasn't even empty, but he said, "I'll have a shot too. Just one, though."

"How restrained of you," I muttered. I couldn't stop thinking of the bad time Ducky was going through. I also couldn't stop thinking that he was our driver. And he had just made a million promises to my father.

"Ducky?" I said, leaning across the table.

"Yeah?" Ducky leaned across the table too, and our heads met in the middle. Then Amalia and Sunny leaned in to hear what was going on.

"Nothing," I replied.

Even later Saturday afternoon 3/6

The shots of tequila arrived, and Ducky and Sunny knocked them back. I have to admit that I didn't _know_ that was what you do with a shot – drink it down in one gulp. IN ONE GULP. I have tasted strong liquor (like tequila) and it's hard enough to sip that stuff. I mean, it's so... so _alcoholic_. It burns your throat and makes your eyes water. How can people chug back a whole big slurp at once?

But that's what Sunny and Ducky did with their shots.

I watched them. I waited for their heads to become disconnected from their necks or something. But nothing much happened. Even so, I felt compelled to try to say something to Ducky again. I waited until Sunny had turned around and was talking to someone she knew from school, and Amalia was watching the warm-up act set up their equipment. Then I said, "Ducky?"

He leaned forward again. "Yeah?"

"You promised my dad you'd be a safe driver."

"I know."

"But you're drinking."

Ducky looked at his watch. "This'll be totally out of my system by the time the concert's over. Trust me."

"Okay."

The truth was that Ducky sounded fine. And he looked fine. So did Sunny. I sat back and decided not to let any of this ruin my evening with Pierre.

Ten minutes later the warm-up act finally began. It was this group of three guys and a girl wearing more ripped clothing than I have ever seen in my life. It was SO ripped that if you'd put it all together it would have made, like, one T-shirt and one pair of jeans.

They sang really loudly and the whole time they sang they jumped up and down. Not bouncing a little in time to the beat but actually jumping, like in gym class. How could they do that and play the instruments at the same time? I looked at Amalia and could see she was trying to figure this out too.

The noise level in the room was rising. The band was growing louder, but not many people were listening to them. They were still trying to talk to each other, so now they were shouting.

Rick returned and brought Sunny and Ducky each another shot of tequila. Ducky looked plenty relaxed to me.

After about 45 minutes the group (whose name I still don't know) played their final song. They ended it with a huge group jump, and one of the guys threw his tambourine to the floor. Then he picked it up and threw it out into the audience. The girl who caught it waved it around over her head, but the room was so deafeningly noisy that you couldn't hear it at all.

The lights came up and a flurry of activity began on the stage. The group removed their instruments and equipment. Then new equipment was set up. It was set up very quickly, and each piece was marked JAX.

A thrill of excitement rushed through me.

When the lights dimmed once again, everybody grew absolutely silent. I thought I could hear Ducky breathing on the other side of the table.

From somewhere behind me an announcer said, "Ladies and gentlemen . . . JAX!"

The room exploded in applause and whistles and cheers. Then it grew quiet again as the members of Jax — three guys and two girls — filed onto the stage. Pierre was the fourth one to appear, and he was the only one who looked out at the audience, looked at us with those piercing, gentle, sincere eyes. Then he looked RIGHT AT ME.

I swear he did.

And he smiled. (At ME.)

A moment later Pierre and the other band members glanced at one another, nodded once, and BLAM! They burst into their first song. It was like the room was so quiet and then all of a sudden it was this fireball of sound. Pierre stood off to the right with one of the girls, and you could tell that as they sang, they just totally lost themselves in the music. Pierre closed his eyes, of course. He always does when he sings. He hardly ever opened them, no matter how much he jumped around (although Jax did not leap up and down the way the warm-up group did). I knew that he had to be off in his own world in order to stay involved with the music.

The first song was loud and wild from beginning to end.

The second song was quiet. It was a ballad, a love song. Pierre sang this one on his own. And his voice was so filled with longing. He told the story of a guy and a girl who fall in love and go off to

London to spend the rest of their lives together. But then the guy falls for another girl and he feels terrible because he realizes he loves both of them. At first he doesn't know what to do, but finally he decides his first love is his true love, except that by then she has found out about the other girl so she leaves the guy and then he has no one.

By the time the song ended I was crying. Tears were just rolling down my cheeks. I soaked through four napkins trying to get control of myself.

Oh, Pierre, I thought. If you and I were those true loves, I wouldn't leave you. Maybe I'd want to have a big talk about faithfulness, and maybe I'd lay down a few ground rules for you to follow, but I wouldn't leave you.

I gulped and sniffled and blew my nose again. Then I looked hard (yet lovingly) at Pierre, hoping he'd open his eyes even just a flicker. I'd send him a message with my own eyes — a message of love and trust to let him know that I wouldn't treat him the way the girl in the song treated him. I mean, the way the girl in the song treated the guy in the song.

Saturday evening 3/6

By the third song, the audience had relaxed a little. We were still under the spell of Jax, but we were no longer transfixed. People began to get up and move around again. (Rick and the girl delivered another shot to our table, but I barely noticed.) The small dance floor in front of the stage started to fill up. I saw people dancing in groups of three or four, or in pairs, or even alone. One guy stood at the edge of the dance floor with his eyes shut, swaying in time to the music for nearly half an hour. Girls danced together, guys danced together, people drifted around and danced with people they didn't know.

For the entire first half of the

concert I was glued to my seat, gazing at Pierre (who rarely opened his eyes). Finally Ducky said to me, "Want to dance, Dawn?" (Sunny was off dancing with someone else, someone I'd never seen before.)

"Sure," I said to Ducky.

We edged through the sea of tables to the dance floor. I'd never danced with Ducky and he turned out to be wild. He was all over the place (at least as much as he could be in that small, crowded area), but he was really good. People turned to look at him. After awhile, I couldn't keep up with him, so when this girl and this guy sort of started dancing with him, I signaled that I was going to head back to our table. When I got there, I found that both Sunny and Amalia were off somewhere. So I sat alone in my seat next to the cluster of shot glasses and lost myself in Pierre's world.

Sitting alone at our end of the table, with most of the people in the room either dancing or just listening to Jax, I could fantasize endlessly about Pierre. I mean, there he was, in the same room, just yards away from me.

This was my best fantasy of the evening:

The concert ends a little earlier than we have figured, which is good because we don't have to call Dad right away.

I say, "Let's go to the back entrance and see if we can see Jax when they leave." Of course, I am thinking that maybe I would get to speak to Pierre.

So we wait by the back door (miraculously, we are the ONLY ones waiting by the back door), and soon the members of Jax start to leave. They are dressed in their regular clothes, which do not look all that different than their concert clothes, but you can tell they are more relaxed and comfortable now.

I look directly into Pierre's eyes and find that he is looking directly into mine.

And we just melt. Both of us.

"Hello," Pierre says to me in his wonderful low voice.

I can barely speak, but I do manage to squeak out, "Hello."

The next thing I know, Pierre is inviting me out for coffee, and we are on our own.

That night he proposes to me.

We go steady until I am old enough to get married.

Meanwhile, I manage his career, and thanks to me he remains wildly successful. We are partners for life.

Late Saturday night 3/6

The concert ended after a mere five minutes. That's how it felt, anyway. So I was surprised to look at my watch and see that it was almost 1:30 A.M.

I was in heaven.

Until the lights came up and I looked across the table at Ducky. I don't know when he had stopped dancing and returned to the table. But at some point he had, and now he was sitting before the shot glasses, his face weary and his eyes glazed.

"Whoa, Ducky," I said quietly.

Ducky looked up at me slowly with hooded eyes. "What?"

"How much did you have to drink?"

Next to him Sunny made a face at me. "Well, let's see," she said. "Let's count the shot glasses. One, two, three, four, five. Five. Five shots of tequila, and Ducky and I were both drinking, so now let's do the math. I had three. Five minus three. My. That's difficult. I almost need a calculator. But—"

"Oh, shut up, Sunny," I muttered.

Sunny shut up.

I looked at Ducky. I looked at Amalia. "Two shots of tequila," I said to her. "Plus that other thing."

Amalia nodded. Then she said, "Ducky, are you wasted?"

Ducky grinned tiredly. "I may not be wasted, but I'm definitely wiped. Maybe I shouldn't have danced so hard... Plus, I was so tired to begin with. I guess that doesn't mix well with a few drinks. Nurse," he said, turning to Sunny. "What time was my last shot?"

"Ducky, this is serious!" I exclaimed.

"Ducky, this is serious!" said Sunny.

"Sunny," I said warningly.

"Sunny," Sunny said warningly.

"Stop that!"

"Stop that!"

"Ducky, she's acting like a six-year-old," I cried.

"Ducky, she's acting like a six-year-old," Sunny cried, then let loose with a belly laugh.

I turned to Amalia. "What are we going to do?"

"What are we going to do?" Sunny asked Amalia.

Amalia took me by the arm and pulled me away from the table. "Let's let Sunny and Ducky calm down a little," she said. "We don't have to leave right away. Maybe we could hang around the back door and wait for Jax. That would be fun, wouldn't it?"

According to my daydream it would be more than fun. But I didn't think we had the time. "Amalia, we can't. I have to call my father and tell him we're on our way home."

"Why? Call him at two and tell him the concert ended then."

I looked at my watch. "That's only twenty minutes from now. Do you really think Ducky will be ready to drive at two o'clock?"

Amalia and I turned to look at Ducky, who was now slumped in one chair with his feet resting on a second chair and his head propped up on his hand. He looked ready to fall asleep. He also, suddenly, looked sad.

Amalia made a little face. "I guess not."

"We have to talk to him," I said.

"Okay. And if Sunny bothers you, just ignore her."

Amalia and I returned to the table and sat down across from Ducky.

"Ducky?" I said. This time Sunny remained quiet.

"Yeah?" said Ducky.

"Are you okay?" Amalia asked him, and I could tell she meant more than simply, "Are you okay to drive?"

The room was emptying out around us, and I watched people slide by as I waited for Ducky's answer.

Sunday morning 3/7

Ducky didn't even lift his head from his hand. "I'm just really tired," he said. "I've probably never been more tired in my life."

Well, he had probably never been so wrung out and emotional and then had a drink plus two shots of tequila, and danced like a madman.

"Do you want to talk about anything?" Amalia asked him gently.

Ducky smiled. "Yes. But not when it's almost two o'clock and I have to get all you guys home."

"*Can* you get us home, Ducky?" I asked. "Are you okay to drive?"

"Of *course* he's okay to drive," spoke up Sunny. "*I* could drive us home right now. And I had more to drink than he did."

"Okay," I said. "A, you are three years away from getting your license, and B, *you* are not in any condition to drive, either. Ducky, do you think you can drive us home?" I asked again.

Ducky looked at the tabletop. "I'm awfully sleepy," he admitted.

"But can you drive?" asked Amalia.

"And I feel like all my bones have slipped out of my body."

"Oh, god," I muttered.

"I guess I better not drive," Ducky finally said.

"*I* could drive!" Sunny said brightly.

Amalia looked at her and rolled her eyes.

"No, really. I could," said Sunny. "I've watched people drive millions of times. And sometimes when my parents aren't home I drive the drive up and down the carway."

I glanced at Amalia. I almost smiled.

"Sunny. Did you hear what you just said?" asked Amalia.

"What?"

"You said 'drive the drive up and down the carway.'"

"Well, you know what I mean."

"Yeah," I answered. "You mean that if you COULD drive — and you can't — you aren't in any condition to."

"And neither am I," Ducky said again.

I almost felt relieved. Relieved that Ducky had admitted this and now we wouldn't have to risk getting in the car with him and _finding out_ that he couldn't drive — but when it was way too late, like when we had just collided with a semi on the freeway. Now, however, I was going to have to call Dad and tell him what bad judgment I'd exercised by thinking that I could trust my pal Ducky, and that Dad was going to have to pay for my bad judgment by getting dressed and driving all the way to North Palo at two in the morning.

Even so, I said, "Well, I have to call Dad now anyway, so I guess I'll ask him to come pick us up. Ducky, you can leave your car here, and you and Ted can drive back tomorrow in Ted's car to get it. It should be okay overnight. Dad's not going to be happy about—"

I stopped talking. Sunny was gaping at me. "What?" I said.

"Are you crazy?" Sunny burst out. "Are you CRAZY?"

"No... What?"

"We are NOT calling your father and asking him to drive here and get us like four little babies. You must be out of your mind."

"You'd rather get in the car with someone who's incapable of driving?" I said hotly to Sunny.

"I *am* really drowsy," interjected Ducky, "and I read somewhere that drowsy drivers cause more accidents than—"

Sunny cut him off. "You can drive just fine," she said. She stood up. "Get up," she ordered Ducky. "Come on. If Dawn doesn't want to come with us she doesn't have to. She can call her father and he can pick HER up, but the rest of us don't have to be humiliated."

"Sunny, keep your voice down!" I cried softly. I had just realized we were the only people left in the room.

Sunny glared at me.

Later Sunday morning 3/7

I wondered if we were going to get kicked out of the club, but when a couple of busboys came into the room a few minutes later, they just started clearing tables and didn't pay any attention to us, which was a good thing, because Sunny started this HUGE fight with me.

"Dawn, quit telling me what to do!" she cried.

At first I couldn't think what I had told her to do. Then I remembered telling her to keep her voice down. "I don't tell you what to do," I said.

"You're *always* telling me what to do — how to dress, how to act, who to hang out with, to visit Mom more often, to be more responsible." Sunny's list went on and on.

It went on for so long that I lost interest and tried to get back to the matter at hand.

"There is no way that I am getting into the car with Ducky at the wheel," I announced as soon as the list was finished.

"Good. I just said you didn't have to. Go call your father. He can pick you up. Amalia and I will go with Ducky. Ducky, you'll be a friend and drive us, won't you?" pleaded Sunny.

"Oh, man," said Ducky sleepily.

I could feel the color drain from my face. Ducky will do absolutely anything for Sunny, and if she begged him to drive, then he'd drive. It was true that *I* didn't have to get in the car with Ducky, but I didn't want *anyone* to get in the car with Ducky, including Ducky.

"Come on, Ducky," said Sunny. "Let's go. Where are your keys?" She tugged at Ducky's arm.

Ducky got to his feet groggily. He reached into his pocket and pulled out first his wallet, then his keys.

Without even thinking (it was ENTIRELY unpremeditated), I grabbed Ducky's keys out of his hand and dropped them into my purse.

Sunny's mouth fell open. The next thing I knew, she had lunged for me. I clutched my purse to my chest and crossed my arms over it. Sunny tried to pry my wrists away from the purse.

"Give it!" she said hoarsely.

"No."

"GIVE. IT."

"No. Absolutely not."

At this point, someone older than the busboys, the manager, maybe, appeared through a door near the stage. "Okay, kids," he said. "The show's over. Move along, now."

I ran for the double doors leading back to the hallway and the front entrance to the club. Sunny was right behind me. Behind her was Amalia, and behind *her*, following more slowly, was Ducky. As soon as we had run through the double doors, Sunny grabbed me from behind. "Give. Me. The. Key ring," she said slowly in this really quiet voice. It scared me a little.

"Forget it, Sunny," I said.

I looked around the vestibule and saw a bank of four pay phones. I ran for them, dropped some change in the first one, and dialed our phone number. I hoped I wasn't going to have to wrestle Sunny during the conversation, but she was now arguing with Ducky on the other side of the hall.

"Dad," I said the moment I heard his voice, "the concert's over and –"

"Did you have fun?"

"Yes, but Dad, you're going to hate this –"

"What is it?" Dad's voice was immediately sharper.

"Ducky's exhausted. He's been having a really hard time lately and he hasn't been sleeping much, so now he thinks he's a little too, um, tired to drive. To drive safely, I mean. So I was wondering if you could come and get us. Ducky will have to come back tomorrow for his car."

There was a horrible silence on Dad's end of the phone. Then he said stiffly, "Very well. Tell me exactly where you are. I'll be there as soon as I can."

I gave Dad directions to the club and hung up the phone.

Even later Sunday morning 3/7

Here is the conversation that followed when I joined Ducky, Amalia, and Sunny again (note that I clutched my purse the entire time):

Me: Okay, Dad's on his way.

Sunny: (Sarcastically.) Fabulous.

Ducky and Amalia: (Looking truly relieved) Good.

Sunny: You can wait for your father, Dawn, but I am going to take a bus home. I am *not* going to ride with him.

Me: You can't take a bus home by yourself in the middle of the night!

Sunny: I refuse to be humiliated by being picked up by your father, Dawn. We'll get lectured all the way home.

Me: Amalia, Sunny can't go home by herself.

Sunny: How are you going to stop me? And anyway, Amalia, Ducky, why do *you* guys want to get lectured by Mr. Schafer? Come with me. Let Dawn go by herself.

Ducky: No way. I don't think I have enough money left for bus fare. Anyway, I am not going to leave Dawn here. It's not safe.

Sunny: But you'd let me go find the bus station by myself?

Ducky: No, I was going to tell you not to go.

Sunny: You were going to tell me not to go? You can't tell me what to do. Nobody can.

Me: You think it's safe for you to wander around in the middle of the night when it isn't safe for anyone else? That you're immune somehow?

Sunny: No. Turn your hearing aid up, Dawn. That isn't what I said. I said that nobody can tell me what to do.

Ducky: Well, technically, Sunny, anyone can tell you what to do. I can tell you to walk home now. But you don't have to decide to do it.

Sunny: (For a moment, just a fleeting moment, Sunny looks hurt and confused before making this incredibly disgusted face.) The point is (she's now speaking as if she's addressing a room of kindergartners), Dawn's father is going to be here in a little while, and if you guys don't want to face the lecture of your lives, then you'd better come with me to find the bus station.

Ducky: (Now sounding really impatient, which is not like him.) Sunny,

I already told you I don't have any money.

Sunny: I can cover you.

Amalia: Are you sure there _is_ a bus at this hour, Sunny?

Sunny: (Hesitating.) No. But there must be. Buses run all the time.

Me: (Now feeling even more disgusted than Sunny looks.) They do not.

Sunny: Do too.

Me: Do not.

Sunday afternoon 3/7

Sunny and I actually got caught up in a do-too-do-not thing while Ducky and Amalia looked on. (Amalia was rolling her eyes.) Since I was afraid Sunny might simply be trying to distract me, I kept my purse clutched to me at all times. Finally Sunny turned to Ducky and Amalia and said to them, "So, are you coming with me or not?"

"Sunny, _no_," said Ducky firmly. (I

have never heard him talk to her that way.) "It's a stupid idea, and I'm practically asleep on my feet."

"Amalia?" said Sunny.

Amalia sighed and rolled her eyes again.

"I can't believe you guys!" exclaimed Sunny. "All right. I'm leaving." She turned and marched out the front door.

"Sunny." (Ducky sounded SO tired.) "You can't go by yourself."

"Then come with me."

"No. This is ridiculous."

"Okay. 'Bye."

"Sunny."

"Make Dawn give you back your keys."

Ducky looked at me.

"I'm NOT giving them back," I said.

"Take. Them. From. Her," said Sunny.

"I can't. And even if I could, I'm not in any condition to drive. That's what started this whole thing, Sunny."

"You know what? You are a *wimp*," Sunny said to Ducky. "You never stand up for yourself. You don't *do* anything. No wonder your friends are a bunch of thirteen-year-old girls. Guys think you're a dweeb, and girls your own age don't even look twice at you."

"Sunny!" I exclaimed.

"Well, it's true."

Ducky cast his eyes to the floor. For a moment no one said a word. Then Sunny glared at the rest of us. "Dawn, are you going to give the keys back?" she finally asked.

"No."

"Okay. Then I'm leaving."

This time no one argued with her.

I said, "And I'm staying."

"I'm staying with her," said Ducky, trying to sound defiant but still looking at the floor.

"Fine." Sunny pushed open the door.

"Hurry along, kids," said a voice from behind us. "Club's closing. Last bus will be leaving soon."

I turned and saw a guy in a blue uniform with a mop and a bucket on wheels.

Amalia and Ducky and I followed Sunny out the door. She never looked back at us, just kept going down the sidewalk. Finally Amalia said, "Oh, I'll go with her. She can't go by herself."

"Amalia—" I started to say.

"It'll be okay. You two stick together. We'll stick together. I'll call you guys tomorrow. And if we miss the bus, I promise I'll call a cab. I'll figure out how to pay for it."

Amalia caught up with Sunny. A moment later Sunny turned back to Ducky and me. "You are lousy friends, both of you," she called to us. "As far as I am concerned, we are no longer friends."

Well, I already knew that Sunny and I weren't friends. But Sunny and Ducky? Did Sunny really mean that? That she and Ducky are no longer friends?

I couldn't worry about it, though. I was much more worried about the stricken look on Ducky's face. I knew how he felt, or I thought I did. He felt the way I would feel if Ducky had said he and I were no longer friends. And if he had just insulted me in the most hurtful way he could think of.

I took Ducky's hand. We sat down on a low wall outside the club. And waited for Dad to arrive.

Later Sunday afternoon 3/7

I tried to talk to Ducky while we waited for Dad. He barely answered me, but he said this was because he was so very tired.

"Sunny didn't mean what she said," I told Ducky.

Ducky had found a small rock. He tossed it from hand to hand.

"She gets crazy sometimes," I tried again.

"I guess."

"You know about her mom and the chemo, right?"

Ducky nodded. But we both knew it wasn't an excuse for the things Sunny had just said.

When I felt that I couldn't pull another word out of Ducky (even though I could think of lots of things to say to him — like, that *I* love Ducky and would never treat him that way), we finally sat silently on the wall. I remembered to remove my funky earrings. A few cars drove down the street, including a police cruiser. A man and a woman walked down the other side of the street. The streetlights were on, of course, so we weren't exactly sitting in the dark. Still, I began to feel creepy. I was pretty relieved when I saw Dad pull up.

Ducky and I jumped to our feet and hurried to the car. I got in the front next to Dad. Ducky climbed in back. I noticed a pail on the seat and had a feeling Dad had put it there for Ducky for barfing purposes, which meant he hadn't believed me when I said that Ducky was just tired.

Dad greeted us with, "Where are the others?"

Ducky started to answer, but I cut him off. "They got a ride with friends," I said quickly. "But I knew you wouldn't want me to do that. And Ducky didn't want me to wait here by myself."

Dad swiveled around and looked at Ducky. "I appreciate that," he said sincerely. "And I appreciate that you were smart enough to speak up when you felt you couldn't drive safely."

"Thank you," said Ducky. He hesitated, then added, "Sir."

"You did the right thing," Dad went on as he started the car.

"Um, thank you," said Ducky again.

"However," said Dad (and I thought, I just KNEW there was going to be a however), "didn't we talk about drinking and driving less than five hours ago?"

"Yes," said Ducky and I.

"And didn't you promise not to do that?"

"Yes," said Ducky.

"And Dawn, didn't you promise that it wouldn't happen?"

"Yes."

"So why did it happen?"

For a moment I was speechless. How was I supposed to answer that stupid question?

"Well," said Ducky from the backseat, "I only had a couple of drinks, and that was several hours ago. I figured it would have worn off by the time the concert was over. But it's so late now, and I'm just so . . . *tired*."

"And how did you get those drinks? You aren't old enough to drink, are you, Christopher?"

"No."

"Well?"

I was beginning to feel awfully embarrassed. I hadn't thought Dad would *grill* Ducky like this, which almost made me laugh — *grill Ducky* — but then I realized why we were in this mess in the first place.

Sunny.

Lately it seems that any time there's

a mess, Sunny seems to have caused it. And I wind up cleaning up after her.

Even later Sunday afternoon 3/7

I am so glad that my grounding ends tomorrow. I don't think I could take much more of this. Dad didn't say I couldn't leave my room, but I've been cooped up in it because Gracie has been crying a lot today and Jeff has two friends over and they've been running around the house like maniacs playing I don't know what, so my room is the only sane place in the house.

I will actually be delighted to go to school tomorrow (even though I'll probably run into Sunny).

When Dad said "Well?" like that to Ducky in the car, I winced. Then I turned around to look at Ducky.

"No, I'm not old enough to drink," said Ducky.

"So how did you get the drinks?"

I answered for Ducky, since I

really didn't see why _he_ should be lectured by my father. I hadn't gotten any further than explaining about the bracelet system when Dad said, "They were _serving_ alcohol at the concert?"

"Well, yes," I replied. "I mean, it's a club. Remember, I told you the concert was going to be held in a club?"

Pause. "Yes."

My conversation with Maggie was coming back to me, and I was glad I had followed her directions.

After another pause Dad said, "So I'm asking you again, Christopher: How did you get the drinks? Were you wearing a bracelet?"

"No," mumbled Ducky.

"Dad, a friend of Ducky's brother just came by and asked if we wanted drinks and then got them for us. _He_ was wearing a bracelet."

"Did _you_ have a drink, Dawn?"

Suddenly I felt like torturing Dad a little. "Yes," I said.

Dad nearly drove off the freeway. "What?" he said quietly.

"I had a seltzer."

Dad narrowed his eyes at me. "Anything else?"

"Nope. Not even another seltzer."

"I can attest to that, sir," spoke up Ducky.

"Well, good," said Dad, but he was shaking his head.

"Dad, I have to say, I really don't understand exactly why you're so mad," I said. "I didn't drink, and Ducky was responsible enough to admit that he couldn't drive and to let me call you, a person who is a safe driver."

This reminded me that Ducky's keys were still in my purse, so I fished them out and handed them to him. Then I looked at Dad, waiting for him to answer me.

All he said was, "We'll discuss this at home."

Monday afternoon 3/8

I'm getting ahead of myself. Or at any rate, my life is getting ahead of my journal. I had thought I'd be able to finish writing about Friday night yesterday. But no, what did Dad suddenly remember at, like, 4:00 yesterday afternoon? My promise to clean out the garage. So I had to put away the journal and spend the next two hours sorting through boxes and bags, piles of stuff that need to go to the recycling center, and dirty, oily tools and gadgets that no one has used in years.

Then, after dinner, it was time for my weekend homework. I suppose I could have started it yesterday morning at the beginning of my grounding, but I was too mad. So I had to do it all last night.

UPDATE: Mrs. Winslow came back from the hospital while I was cleaning the garage. She rode in the ambulance again.

Seeing Mrs. Winslow made me think

of Sunny. This mess — the concert, Ducky, Dad, being grounded — is basically her fault. I'm not even going to wonder why she's so wild. I know why. Because of her mother. Carol and I have talked about this endlessly. Okay. That's why she's wild. But why is she cruel, thoughtless, and basically just a bad friend? She was so mean to Ducky on Friday night — Ducky, who loves her and looks out for her and at the moment is just as vulnerable as she is. Why did she do that?

And why did she insist on drinking and pulling Ducky into that with her? From the second we entered the club, all she could think about was getting a drink. The first thing she wanted to do was buy a bracelet. She probably would have stolen one if she'd had the opportunity.

I DO NOT UNDERSTAND SUNNY.

Five minutes later

But I still wish we were best friends again.

Monday night 3/8

Back to Friday night.

I noticed the most interesting thing as Dad was driving us down the freeway back to Palo City.

It was Ducky.

Now, if _I_ were being driven along and lectured by the father of one of my friends I would be either absolutely livid or unspeakably embarrassed, but Ducky seemed . . . actually, he seemed kind of relieved. Even _pleased_. At first I couldn't figure out why, but now that I've had time to think about it, I've decided it's because Ducky's own parents can't do this for him. I know he thinks his parents don't care about him and Ted very much. They're in another country, for god's sake, and have left Ducky and Ted on their own. So when Ducky does something wrong, well, that's it. Nothing *happens*. Ted isn't going to punish him. And chances are, his parents will never know he *did* anything wrong. So maybe it's kind of refreshing for Ducky to be lectured by a parent (even someone else's parent) when he's messed up.

At long last, Dad pulled into Ducky's driveway. His parting words, as Ducky was opening the back door of our car, were something about alcoholism. Ducky just said, "Yes, sir," kind of saluted Dad, and then let himself into his house.

I don't think Ted was home.

Poor Ducky.

It's funny. Dad was being all lecture-y and stern, but he didn't do the one thing I'd been sure he'd do. He didn't ask to have a word with Ted when we reached the McCraes' house. He knew Mr. and Mrs. McCrae weren't there, but I guess he realized that even Ted wasn't there and Ducky was on his own.

Maybe Dad will take Ducky under his wing.

Or not.

Two minutes later

Just reread last entry. Another duck pun. Couldn't help it.

Later Monday night 3/8

Dad and I were pretty quiet as we drove to our house. It was 3:00 when we finally parked the car in the garage. To my surprise, Carol was up waiting for us. She'd made tea. She and Dad and I sat around the kitchen table and talked. Neither Dad nor Carol seemed particularly angry. Still, I wasn't surprised when they told me I was grounded for the rest of the weekend. It had something to do with choosing my friends and not begging to put myself in situations that were basically too old for me. Man, I hope they never find out about the party at Ms. Krueger's house.

Finally, just after 3:30, we all went to bed.

Despite the bad end to our night, I went to bed and dreamed of Pierre. We were on this beach, holding hands . . .

Tuesday afternoon 3/9

For some reason, the days are dragging by. Well, of course, Saturday and Sunday dragged because of my being grounded and stuck in the house. And cleaning the garage was no picnic. It only took two hours, but they felt like eight. I must speak with Maggie about the "bribing" aspect of her scheme. It may not work for everybody.

The last two days have been pretty draggy too. I just feel so bad for Ducky.

When I got to school yesterday

morning Maggie and Amalia pounced on me right away. I hadn't spoken to Amalia since her call Saturday, and Carol had only taken phone messages from Maggie. (I was sure Maggie and Amalia had spoken to each other, though.)

"Are you still grounded?" was Maggie's greeting.

"Nope. It's over." I twisted the dial on my locker.

"What happened over the weekend?" asked Amalia.

"Nothing. And I mean NOTHING," I replied. "It was the quietest, most boring weekend on record. I wrote in my journal, did my homework, and cleaned out the garage. Period. Have you guys spoken to Sunny?"

"I talked to her yesterday," said Maggie. "Boy, was she mad."

"At me?" I asked.

"Mostly."

"But she was the one with the stupid idea of getting drinks for Ducky. Our driver."

"I didn't say she was *right*," said Maggie.

"Besides, she was also really mad at Ducky," added Amalia.

"At Ducky? Why?" I asked.

"Well . . . I think because he took your side on Friday night. He agreed with you that he shouldn't drive. And then he waited with you for your father to pick you up."

I pulled two books out of my locker, then slammed the door shut. "Well, *I'm* really mad at Sunny. Ducky should be too," I said.

At that very moment, Ducky materialized behind Maggie. He was wearing that baseball cap again, with the bill pointing left.

Maggie turned and saw him. "What's with the hat?" she asked.

"It's protecting me from Sunny," he replied. "As long as I'm wearing this, she has no power in my immediate universe."

"Why do you need protection from Sunny?" asked Amalia.

Ducky just looked at her. "Amalia."

"Okay, okay. It's just that I don't think she'll *stay* mad at you."

Ducky looked hopeful. "You don't? Then maybe she *isn't* still mad at me. I haven't seen her yet."

Later Tuesday afternoon 3/9

Sunny was most definitely still mad at Ducky. But we didn't discover this until later in the morning. Classes were changing and Ducky and I were talking in the hall for a minute. I spotted Sunny walking toward us and I nudged Ducky.

"Hey, Sunny," said Ducky brightly as she approached us.

Sunny glanced at Ducky, then glanced away and passed by us without a word. The look on Ducky's face was just awful.

He removed the cap and put it in his pocket.

I could have killed Sunny.

"It'll be okay," I told Ducky.

"Yeah," he said.

Tuesday night 3/9

Mrs. Winslow went back to the hospital today. Back and forth. Back and forth. It must be horrible for her.

And for Sunny.

At the moment I don't have a lot of sympathy for Sunny, though. She could make her ordeal easier by letting us be her friends again. But she won't. She keeps pushing us away.

I can't believe she's pushing Ducky away now too.

Wednesday afternoon 3/10

Looking out my window, and there's Ducky. He's just standing on the sidewalk in front of Sunny's house.

Wednesday evening 3/10

When I saw Ducky I opened our front door and called to him. We sat around and talked for awhile. He was hoping to see Sunny, of course. And at that moment something occurred to me.

"Ducky," I said, "what happened to your after-school job? Aren't you supposed to be working at Sunny's father's store?"

(What had occurred to me was that I'd seen Ducky around in the afternoons an awful lot — and I had just remembered that he worked in the afternoons. Or he used to.)

Ducky mumbled something about quitting the job.

"When?" I asked.

"A month ago. Maybe more."

"Why?"

"All this stuff. Alex. You know."

I tried to understand. "Didn't you like working?"

"It was just too much. Too much pressure. Too much everything. And think how embarrassing it would be if I worked there now."

"Why? Because of running into Sunny?"

"Yeah."

"Huh." I made a face. "You wouldn't run into her there, Ducky. She's never at home, never at the store, and hardly ever at the hospital. Mostly she's wherever her parents aren't."

Ducky sighed. "I thought she kind of relied on me," he said. "I didn't think she'd turn away from me too."

"Carol has a theory," I said.

"And just remember I can hear you from the kitchen!" Carol called to us.

"I'll try to be accurate," I called back. Then I said to Ducky, "Carol's theory is that if Sunny pushes us away first, then we can't leave her. Technically. Is that right, Carol?"

"Technically," she replied.

"Well, it doesn't hurt any less," said Ducky.

"I know."

The phone rang then, and a moment

later Carol poked her head into the living room and said, "Dawn, it's Maggie."

"I'll get the cordless phone," I told her.

I walked around in the living room while I talked to Maggie. Ducky examined a ceramic dolphin and then the hole at the knee of his jeans. He looked bored.

After a few minutes Maggie said, "So do you want to go to the Square after school tomorrow?"

"The Square?" I replied. "Sure." Ducky looked up with interest. "Ducky, do you want to go to the Square with us tomorrow?" I asked.

Ducky looked a teeny bit less bored. "Why not?"

"Maggie, Ducky's going to come too," I said into the phone.

Cafeteria, Thursday 3/11

Lunchtime. Sunny is not in school today. She probably skipped.

Thursday evening 3/11

We had so much fun at the Square today. It was different going with Ducky, though. Partly because he's a guy, and partly because he's Ducky. And slightly depressed. Maggie and I saw it as our job to cheer him up. (Speaking of jobs, I think he should get his back.)

Differences caused by having Ducky along this afternoon:

1. Extreme window shopping. (Ducky practically lives for it.)

2. More $ at end of afternoon. (Ducky paid our bill at the Tea Shop and also bought me a CD. It was on sale, but still.)

3. Covered more ground. (Ducky likes looking in stores but he doesn't

like to stay in them long, so we went to, like, 2,000 of them.)

4. Accumulated more flyers than usual. (Ducky CANNOT say no to a person who holds a flyer out to him.)

5. Laughed more. (Ducky is SO funny, even when he's down.)

6. Ended the afternoon more wound up than when we'd started. (Sometimes Ducky seems like a taut rubber band. The slightest little thing sets him going BOING BOING BOING, and soon Maggie and I were going BOING BOING BOING too.)

Ducky MUST settle down.

I.e., he MUST straighten things out with Sunny, one way or another.

And he could use that job.

And he could probably use his parents too.

Once again — poor Ducky.

Later Thursday evening 3/11

I think somewhere earlier in this

journal I wrote "Desolation." I think it was for something stupid like not getting tickets to see Pierre and Jax.

I didn't know. I didn't know what desolation *really* is. I'll never write something shallow like that again.

I feel like an old, old person.

And now I know why Sunny cut school.

When I came home this afternoon — all happy and wound up from spending the afternoon with Maggie and Ducky — Carol was sitting in the kitchen with Mrs. Bruen, looking very serious.

"Dawn, I want to talk to you," she said.

She sounded *so* serious that at first I thought I was in trouble for something. I thought back over the last few weeks and wondered what I'd done. Finally I said, "Were our report cards sent out?"

Carol frowned. "No. Should I be worried about your report card?"

"No. It's just that . . . What's wrong?"

Mrs. Bruen slipped out of the kitchen then, and I sat down across the table from Carol. "Honey, it's Mrs. Winslow," she began.

"I know. She's back in the hospital."

"Well, actually she's at home again. She came home this morning."

"Oh. Isn't that good news?"

Carol reached across the table and took my hand. "Honey, Mrs. Winslow won't be returning to the hospital."

I didn't understand. "Ever? What do you mean?"

"Sunny's father has arranged for round-the-clock nursing for Mrs. Winslow. At home."

Carol was trying to tell me something and I just wasn't getting it. "Okay," I said finally.

"And there really isn't anything more the doctors can do for Mrs. Winslow. She isn't going to get well, Dawn."

At last I understood. Or thought I did. "You mean — You mean Mrs. Winslow has come home to *die*?"

Most people would have found a way to soften what I had said. But not Carol. And I appreciated that.

"Well," said Carol. "Yes. I suppose she has."

"Oh god, oh god, oh god," I said. I put my forehead on my arm.

Carol stood up and moved to my side of the table. She held me while I cried, and she didn't say much.

Finally, when I sort of had control of myself, I said, "I never thought she would die from this. I really thought she would get better. Even after they stopped the chemo."

"I know," said Carol.

And then I realized why Sunny had cut school.

"God, poor Sunny," I said. "She wasn't in school today, Carol. She must have known this was going to happen. I bet she stayed at home to be with her mother." Either that or she was somewhere else so she wouldn't have to be with her mother.

"Maybe you should call Sunny," Carol suggested.

For some reason that brought on a fresh wave of tears. When I calmed down again I said, "It's no good. I've tried talking to her."

"But maybe she'll talk now. This is different."

"You mean she really needs her friends?" I said. Carol nodded. "But she really needed us before. Why should this be different?"

"Because now it's real," Carol replied.

Extremely late Thursday night 3/11

I can't sleep. I've been trying for hours. All I can think about are Sunny and Mrs. Winslow.

After dinner tonight I called Ducky, then Maggie, then Amalia. I told each of them about Sunny's mother. "Carol thinks Sunny might want to be friends with us again," I told Ducky. He seemed uncertain but said he'd try to talk to her in school tomorrow.

To Maggie and Amalia I said simply, "Sunny really needs us right now."

We all kind of agreed that NO MATTER WHAT Sunny's reaction to us was, we would rally around her.

We would MAKE her be our friend again, and then we would stick with her through the worst, until things got better again, and forever. Because that's what friends do.

Cafeteria, Friday 3/12

Sunny isn't making this easy for us. Of course, she doesn't know about our plan, so how could she oblige us?

At any rate, she's not in school today.

Still lunchtime but later, Friday 3/12

Maggie and Amalia are here now. (I was alone when I wrote the last entry.) And Amalia thinks Sunny _is_ in school.

"But she's not in her classes," I said.

"Well, I passed her in the hall," Amalia replied.

I looked at Maggie, who shrugged. "_I_ haven't seen her," she said.

"Are you sure it was Sunny?" I asked Amalia.

"Positive."

"Where was she?"

"Coming out of Ms. Krueger's office."

Got to go. Lunch is over.

3 secs. between classes, Friday 3/12

Just saw Sunny myself. She _is_ here. But not going to classes. Think I'll camp out by her locker at the end of the day and just wait.

Friday evening 3/12

I waited at Sunny's locker for 15 minutes after the last bell rang. Ducky joined me, then Maggie, then Amalia. The halls had pretty much cleared out.

"Well?" I said finally. I looked around at my friends.

"Well," said Ducky.

The four of us stood up.

"Now what?" asked Amalia.

I sighed. "I guess we go home."

"But we keep after her," said Maggie. "We aren't going to let her get away from us. She has to know we're here for her."

"No matter what it takes," said Ducky.

Friday night 3/12

We haven't heard from Sunny. None of us has. But now the light is on in her room. I can see it from my window.

It's much too late to call her, but tomorrow I will go next door.

Saturday afternoon 3/13

I'm sitting at my desk, looking out my window, and Sunny has just come outside. She's sitting on her back stoop.

Oh god. I think she's crying.

It's time for me to go to her.

Saturday night 3/13

My heart was pounding SO LOUDLY as I walked across our backyard and into Sunny's yard. I barely even noticed how warm it was, unusually warm for March. All I could think about was Sunny. She was sitting on the top of the stoop, kind of hunched over. Her shoulders were shaking. I know she saw me coming, but she didn't say anything. She didn't leave, though, either, and that was a good sign.

I had no idea what to say, so I just sat down next to her. When she didn't move, I put my arm across her shoulders. She still didn't move, so we sat like that for awhile. After a long time (well, it felt like a long time), Sunny's shoulders stopped shaking. She lifted her head and looked at me.

"I guess you heard," she said.

I nodded. "Carol told me."

"And?"

I wasn't sure what Sunny wanted me to say. "And . . . well, I didn't understand at first. But now I do. I cried for a long time."

Sunny nodded. "They don't know how long it will be. I mean, how long . . . Mom will live. Maybe a few weeks. Maybe a couple of months."

I turned around and glanced at the door behind us. Sunny looked too. We couldn't see inside, but Sunny said, "There's a nurse here right now. There are three or four of them and they rotate shifts. I feel like I'm living at the hospital."

"It must be horrible."

"It's pretty bad." Sunny poked at a pebble with her toe. Then she looked at me. "Dawn, I'm really sorry," she said.

"That's okay." I wasn't sure it really was, but I didn't know what else to say at the moment. I think what I meant was that I knew it would be okay. Eventually.

"I know I've been, well . . ."

"Mean?" I suggested. I couldn't help it. I knew Sunny was hurting, but she had hurt me too. Badly. And I wanted her to know that. If she weren't my best friend, I guess it wouldn't have mattered so much. But she was my best friend. Even after everything that had happened.

"Have I been mean?" asked Sunny.

"Sometimes."

"I'm sorry. I've really missed you."

"I've missed you too. But you kept pushing me away."

"I know."

I didn't press Sunny for an explanation. I was sure Carol had been right. Anyway, the point was that Sunny had missed me.

And I thought perhaps she needed me now. It had been a long time since she had confided her feelings in me. Surely that meant something. I decided I was willing to try on our friendship again. I'd been without it for so long that I'd forgotten just what it felt like, only that it used to be wonderful.

"Maybe we could forget about the last few months," I said. As if that were possible. It seemed like a good thing to say, though. And if we both tried very, very hard . . .

"Really?"

I nodded. "Yeah."

"Okay."

"Just promise me something."

"What?" said Sunny warily.

"That the next time you're sad or upset, instead of disappearing, call me. Or come over. Or call Maggie or Amalia."

"Or Ducky?" said Sunny.

"Definitely Ducky."

"He called this morning."

"Did you talk?"

"A little. It was hard because things were kind of busy here. But he's coming over later."

"Ducky loves you, you know, Sunny. He thinks of you as his sister."

"I know."

I smiled at Sunny. She smiled back. It was a sad smile, but still.

"Do you want to see Mom?" Sunny asked me.

"Okay," I replied.

We stood up. Then we put our arms around each other and walked into Sunny's house.

Ann M. Martin

About the Author

ANN MATTHEWS MARTIN was born on August 12, 1955. She grew up in Princeton, NJ, with her parents and her younger sister, Jane.

Although Ann used to be a teacher and then an editor of children's books, she's now a full-time writer. She gets the ideas for her books from many different places. Some are based on personal experiences. Others are based on childhood memories and feelings. Many are written about contemporary problems or events.

All of Ann's characters are made up. But some of her characters are based on real people. Sometimes Ann names her characters after people she knows; other times she chooses names she likes.

In addition to California Diaries, Ann Martin has written many other books, including the Baby-sitters Club series. She has written twelve novels for young people, including *Missing Since Monday, With You or Without You, Slam Book,* and *Just a Summer Romance.*

Ann M. Martin does not live in California, though she does visit frequently. She lives in New York with her cats, Gussie, Woody, and Willy. Her hobbies are reading, sewing, and needlework — especially making clothes for children.

CALIFORNIA DIARIES

Look for #12

Sunny, Diary Three

I DON'T UNDERSTAND. WHY DO PEOPLE HAVE TO DIE? ALL RIGHT, THAT'S A STUPID QUESTION. THEY HAVE TO DIE BECAUSE IF EVERYONE LIVED, AND BABIES KEPT ON BEING BORN, THE WORLD WOULD HAVE BECOME OVERCROWDED A LONG, LONG TIME AGO.

OKAY, WHY DO GOOD, YOUNG PEOPLE HAVE TO DIE? WHY DOES MOM HAVE TO DIE NOW? WHY COULDN'T SHE DIE WHEN SHE'S REALLY, REALLY OLD, THE WAY MOST PEOPLE DO?

I AM NOT READY FOR MOM TO DIE. AND THERE'S NOT A THING I CAN DO ABOUT IT.

THIS IS UNFAIR, UNFAIR, UNFAIR.

I DON'T WANT MOM TO LEAVE YET.

8:20 P.M.

I got called down to dinner. When Aunt Morgan calls, you obey. Actually, I was kind of relieved to close up the journal and do something mundane, like eat.

Aunt Morgan is not much of a cook. Or a housekeeper. But she saw it as her duty to fly out here and take care of Dad and me. So she worked really hard this afternoon to make supper for the three of us. She made a vegetable lasagna. It was runny, overcooked on the top, and undercooked in the middle. It took her a long time to make it. I am trying to be appreciative.

Dad and Aunt Morgan and I ate in the kitchen with the door into Mom's room open so she could hear us. I think Mom was asleep the whole time, though. Already I don't remember much about dinner. Only that I wasn't hungry, but that I forced some of the lasagna down. And I tried to answer Dad's and Aunt Morgan's questions about school and stuff.

Then I just looked at the two of them sitting there, all defeated. After a few moments, I excused myself.

Why has everyone given up on Mom?

I want to yell, "DON'T GIVE UP! DON'T GIVE UP!" I even want to yell those words at Mom. Because she has given up too. I know she has. And I don't understand why.

Also, I don't want the end to come. I am not ready.